Acknowledgments

Much thanks to my brilliant, dedicated agent and friend, Dave Dunton, and also to my truly fantastic editor, Megan McKeever. I cannot say enough good things about either of them, and I'm extremely grateful for their guidance. Huge thanks also to Lauren McKenna, Erica Feldon, Louise Burke, and Sarah Self for all their excellent work and support, as well as Carrie Beck, Regina Starace, Jane Elias, Susan Lewis, Ryan Gattis, Manish Kalvakota, Matt O'Keefe, Leah Stewart, Bobby and Sarah McCain, Nikki Van De Car, Pamela Cooper, my mom and dad, and my parents-in-law. Much love to my wife and co-conspirator, Lisa.

oblivion road

oblivion road

A NOVEL

Alex McAulay

Pocket Books   MTV Books
New York   London   Toronto   Sydney

Pocket Books
A Division of Simon & Schuster, Inc.
1230 Avenue of the Americas
New York, NY 10020

MTV Music Television and all related titles, logos, and characters are trademarks of MTV Networks, a division of Viacom International Inc.

First MTV Books/Pocket Books trade paperback edition November 2007

POCKET and colophon are registered trademarks of Simon & Schuster, Inc.

For information about special discounts for bulk purchases, please contact Simon & Schuster Special Sales at 1-800-456-6798 or business@simonandschuster.com.

Designed by Mary Austin Speaker

Manufactured in the United States of America

10 9 8 7 6 5 4 3 2 1

ISBN-13: 978-1-4165-4806-5
ISBN-10:   1-4165-4806-8

For Lisa

The dark-haired girl sprawled unconscious in the deep snow, the soft moonlight giving her pale features a fine glow, like an image from a fairy tale. Her hair fanned out around her head like folds of silk as the heavy snow continued to fall. Her clothes were already covered, as was one of her hands. The stark whiteness of the snow was marred only by drops of red that had come from her nose and ears.

Clutching his arm to his chest, as though it were broken, a teenage boy stumbled onto the two-lane road where the girl lay. He had struggled up from the ditch at the edge of the forest. Now he waded through the snow toward the girl, panting for air. Everything was white and silent, the road completely deserted. The boy knelt down by the girl's side and saw how still and quiet she was.

Seemingly afraid to hurt her, he put a hand out and gently touched her snow-covered shoulder. Then he started saying her name.

When he first tried to wake her, the girl was still deep in a dream. She didn't want to wake up. Inside the dream she was safe, but she knew that if she woke up, she'd have to face the terrible thing that had just happened to her. She also knew somehow that outside the dream it was bitterly cold. The kind of cold that could suck the breath from your lungs and freeze the hairs in your nose. She would do anything to avoid feeling like that again.

But the boy's intrusive voice wouldn't stop calling for her. Over and over she heard her name, and she fought against it.

Suddenly, the hands touching her became rougher and she felt herself being pulled back into the harsh reality of her present surroundings. She curled up, keeping her eyes tightly shut.

"You're bleeding," she heard the voice say. "Your nose." Although she couldn't place the voice, it sounded familiar.

She supposed that now she was awake, she might as well give up and open her eyes. But when she tried, they wouldn't open all the way, like they were swollen or had sleep dirt in them. *Eye boogers,* she'd called the dirt when she was a little kid.

She finally got her eyes partway open and was somewhat surprised to see where she was. She was lying right in the middle of the desolate, snow-covered road. The snow was almost two feet deep.

"What happened?" she tried to ask as she sat up, but the words came out as a muffled burr. She reached a hand up and brushed snow and blood away from her nose and mouth. Her hand was shaking, and her left shoulder hurt like she'd been punched.

"Courtney, are you okay?" The voice was panicked, trembling with concern.

"Yeah," she mumbled. But she felt far from okay. Her head was aching like her brain wanted to burst out of the confines of her skull, and she felt dizzy, as though she'd drunk too much cough syrup. She brushed more snow off her face and out of her hair as she struggled to remember what had happened to her. When she looked down at her hand there was a lot of blood on it. "I feel sick."

Vague memories flitted at the edges of her mind. Some of them seemed silly, and some seemed important. She had been inside a car, an SUV. She remembered it had smelled like French fries because they'd stopped for fast food at a drive-thru a few hours earlier. She tried to focus her mind on more crucial issues: Where was the car now? Where had they been coming back from? Where had they been going? Most of all, she wondered what had happened to her, and if she'd be okay.

Courtney heard a noise as the boy sat down heavily in the snow next to her, looking dazed. In her confused state, she'd nearly forgotten about him. His tousled brown hair was matted with blood and dirt, and he had small cuts all over his face. They were tiny, like paper cuts. His eyes were very frightened, the pupils wide in the moonlight. For a second, she couldn't remember who he was, and it scared her. She knew she was supposed to know. Then his name came rushing back.

"Jeremy!" she said, relieved. He was her friend. From high school.

She moved sideways in the snow and hugged him, feeling his warmth. He put his arms around her, and she winced in pain.

"I thought you might be dead," he finally said. She could hear the emotion in his voice. "I couldn't get you to wake up."

"It's okay . . ." Her vision went all blurry for a second, but then it cleared again. "What happened to us?"

"You don't remember?"

She shook her head, but it hurt her neck, so she stopped. "No. I mean, sort of." Her memory of the event was slowly coming back. She remembered they'd been returning from a ski trip at Quail Ridge Run outside Pagosa Springs. They had spent a weekend there at a condo owned by Jeremy's father. It was now the tail end of Christmas break, and they were supposed to have left earlier in the day, but they'd stayed late. The boys had wanted one final run on a slope, a double diamond that had scared her.

"We had an accident," Jeremy said. "We crashed the SUV."

Courtney swallowed hard. "Oh my God." She turned to him slowly, trying not to make the pain worse. "Are we going to be okay?"

"I think so. You—" Jeremy broke off. He looked away at the snow. "I think you got thrown out of the car. I just found you here on the road."

Courtney supposed she should be horrified, but she felt too numb to process his words. She looked down at her legs and made sure that she could move them. She could, although her body felt battered and bruised. She thought to herself: *I could have died.* She realized the snow had probably protected her and softened her landing. She felt glad to be alive, but oddly detached. She guessed the emotions would hit her later.

Courtney heard a strange choking sound and realized that Jeremy had started crying.

"Don't cry," she said. She had never seen him cry before, and they had been friends for well over two years, since the start of ninth grade.

"How are the others?" Courtney asked. She said it partly to distract him, because she didn't know what else to do. To be honest, she couldn't fully remember yet who had been on the trip.

"They're still in the SUV." Jeremy wiped his eyes. His hair was getting covered in snowflakes. "I climbed out my window to get help on the road. I found you first. We have to go back for them."

Courtney wiped some more blood from the corner of her nose as Jeremy got to his feet.

"Can you stand up?"

"I don't know." She gave Jeremy her arms, and he helped her up. The snow was so deep it came to her knees. Her ankles hurt, but the pain was bearable. She put an arm around Jeremy's shoulders for balance.

Courtney felt as though she'd taken a detour from real life and ended up someplace terrifying. She had no idea what stretch of road this was, only that it was cold and abandoned. Even though she was trying, she still couldn't remember anything about the accident. The last thing she remembered was laughing about some stupid pop song on the radio, turning around to look at Reyna—

Her thoughts veered off as she realized what that meant. It meant that Reyna Foster, her best friend since junior high, had been on the trip with them. And now there was no sign of her. Courtney gripped the sleeve of Jeremy's thin jacket.

"Reyna . . ." she said.

He nodded grimly. "Yeah."

There was nothing more for either of them to say. Courtney didn't want to give voice to thoughts that were too horrible to face. She told herself that if she was okay, and Jeremy was okay, then Reyna probably would be too.

Courtney and Jeremy began to hobble through the snow to the edge of the road, where the ditch waited. It was wide and deep, a massive crevice overhung by snow-weighted tree branches. Everything was white.

"How did we crash?" Courtney asked as they stumbled forward.

"We hit a deer. A big one." He paused. "We started rolling and I blacked out. When I woke up, the SUV was in the woods. My door wouldn't open and no one answered me. I didn't know what to do."

"So the others are still inside the car? You're sure about that?"

"I think so." It sounded like he was in shock.

Courtney wondered what the SUV looked like now. She knew it had to be bad if she'd been tossed from the wreckage. She was incredibly lucky to have survived.

Courtney and Jeremy paused at the shoulder of the road, where the earth dropped away. The ditch seemed impossibly deep, and there was no guardrail. The snow disoriented Courtney, and she couldn't tell exactly where the road ended and the edge of the steep slope began.

She was very conscious of the cold. Every part of her that was exposed felt the sting of the freezing night air. She didn't have a jacket on, only a wool sweater, jeans, and boots. She shivered, rubbing her aching, throbbing arms, trying to stay warm.

"We slid off the road," Jeremy said. He pointed back behind them. "Those are our tire tracks, but the snow's filling them fast. I don't even know how long it's been since we crashed." He stared into the ditch. "The SUV's down there somewhere."

Courtney and Jeremy began picking their way down

the snow-covered slope. Courtney was afraid she might fall, but she knew she had to focus and stay calm. Everything still had the strange, dislocated feeling of a nightmare. She clutched Jeremy's arm.

As they got closer to the bottom, where the snow and foliage were deeper and thicker, she saw signs of the SUV. Ahead of them, a ragged gap had been plowed through the underbrush and trees, like a hole punched right through the pristine landscape. Courtney realized the SUV had slid down the embankment and kept going, into the forest beyond, and was now hidden.

What if the others are dead? She tried to push the thought out of her mind.

"We need to get to the SUV." Every word Courtney spoke sounded like it had a slight delay, like she was hearing someone else's words coming from her mouth. She wondered if she had a concussion. She brought a hand up to her head and found two separate lumps that were starting to swell. It hurt to even graze them with her numb fingertips. "I can't believe this happened to us," she murmured softly.

Jeremy nodded, but he looked distracted. Courtney noticed one of his hands was pressed up against his side.

"You okay?" she asked him.

"Sure." But he didn't sound okay. He sounded like he was in pain.

"What's wrong?"

"I got a stitch, or a cramp. Or something. I'll be fine."

Courtney could tell he was trying to be stoic, like boys were supposed to act. But she'd already seen him cry, so she wished he would just be honest with her.

The two of them walked through the snow at the bottom of the ditch until they reached the gap in the trees. It appeared as though the SUV had possibly crashed through on its side or on its roof. Courtney didn't allow herself to wonder what kind of shape her friends were in. Her fingers were feeling so numb it was scaring her, so she blew on them and rubbed them. She didn't know where her gloves had gone.

The hole left by the car opened onto a spectral, crystalline world, and Courtney peered inside, caught between awe and terror. Trees that had been sheared by the impact were already getting covered with snow again. There was dead, utter silence.

"Look," Courtney said. In the distance, thirty yards or more into the white forest, were the remains of the SUV. The car had come to rest at the base of a thick pine tree. It was right-side up, but looked half crumpled, like a discarded piece of construction paper. Random items from inside were scattered on the forest floor atop the snow, black shadows in the half-light. Courtney could see shattered glass and bits of metal glistening along the path to the car. Most of the windows, except the front windshield, looked completely broken out.

Courtney's first thought was that it didn't look like the kind of accident people could survive. She glanced over at Jeremy, and he looked as stunned as she felt.

"Fuck," he said, the word coming out in a breathy exhalation. She noticed he was still holding his side. "It's worse than I remembered."

Without saying another word, they began moving toward the car as quickly as they could. Courtney pushed branches out of her way as she stumbled forward, getting covered in even more snow. The snow infiltrated her sweater and her jeans, yet she barely registered the sensation.

She reached the SUV first, a moment before Jeremy. "Reyna!" she called out. And then, her memory returning in a final burst, "Harris! Melanie!" Courtney remembered now there had been five of them in all. She, Reyna, Jeremy, and then Harris and Melanie: two friends of Jeremy's from his church youth group who happened to be a couple. They'd come along on the ski trip too. She didn't know them that well, but they'd all had a good time together, skiing and partying in Pagosa Springs.

I just can't believe things ended up this way, Courtney thought.

Jeremy moved behind Courtney and went past her, starting to yell out names too. At first, there was no response from inside the SUV. Courtney was trying to think about where everyone had been sitting. She knew Jeremy had been driving—it was his parents' Ford Explorer—and she'd been sitting next to him up front. But Reyna had been in the backseat with Harris and Melanie.

Courtney tugged on the doors and tried to get inside,

but couldn't. The car had been reconfigured by the accident, all the doors and windows jumbled into one another, like it had been through a trash compactor. Automatically, Courtney kept calling the names of her friends over and over. Jeremy was doing the same, a distant echo now at the far side of the vehicle.

Courtney was almost startled to hear a voice suddenly answer from inside the SUV. "Court?" she heard it say weakly. "Is that you?" The voice belonged to Reyna.

"It's me!" Courtney said, the words tumbling out in relief. Even if Reyna was injured, at least she was still alive, and that was what mattered most. "You're going to be okay. We'll get you out. Are you hurt?"

"I can't tell," Reyna's voice came back. "But I think I'm trapped in here."

"Reyna, don't move," Jeremy said from the other side of the car. "I'm going to pry open the door."

"Do it fast. It's kind of hard to breathe."

Courtney still couldn't see Reyna even though she was looking through one of the broken passenger windows. The interior of the SUV was just too dark. She heard Jeremy grappling unsuccessfully with the door.

"Harris and Mel are in here with me," Reyna managed to add. "They're knocked out, but they're breathing."

Courtney supposed she should be relieved everyone was still alive, against the odds, but she was scared. They were in the middle of nowhere, off some rural road cutting through the countryside from Pagosa Springs up to Denver. It was a thin, winding road between two mountains, a shortcut that Jeremy had seen on the map and insisted they take for some reason. They'd been lost before they crashed, she now remembered that much. Harris and Jeremy had been arguing over which road would get them home fastest.

Jeremy came over to Courtney, gripping trees for balance. His face was very pale. "I can't get the door open."

Although Courtney was in pain, especially from her throbbing head, she forced herself to ignore it. She knew they had to get Reyna and the others out of the SUV, that their friends were depending on her and Jeremy to rescue them. She looked at Jeremy, his hand still clutching his side. Neither of them were in good shape, but Reyna, Harris, and Melanie probably had it worse. She swallowed back fear, trying to think of the right thing to do as she stared at the SUV.

"Listen," she said finally. "I have a plan."

II

Twenty minutes later, the SUV was empty, just a carcass discarded in the forest. Courtney had managed to squeeze inside, through a window, and kick open one of the side doors. They'd rescued Reyna first, unclasping her seat belt and helping her out into the cold. She was shaken and scared, just like Courtney, but mostly unhurt.

Reyna hugged Courtney and Jeremy when she got out, and then she sat down in the snow, taking deep breaths. Her short, curly hair was disheveled, and her dark skin looked paler than Courtney had ever seen it before.

"Man . . ." Reyna said as she checked herself for injuries, listening in horror as Courtney told her about being thrown from the vehicle. It didn't seem like words could do their situation much justice. "The seat belt almost broke my collarbone," Reyna finally said, rubbing her neck. But she didn't stay sitting for long. She got up and helped Courtney and Jeremy in their effort to get Harris and Melanie outside. Courtney was worried about moving either of them in case they had internal injuries, but there wasn't much choice.

They pulled Melanie out before Harris. She moaned a few times, but she didn't regain consciousness as they laid her down on the snow. She looked oddly peaceful, but Courtney knew it was only an illusion. She wondered if this was how she'd looked when Jeremy found her. One of Melanie's legs appeared crooked in her jeans, down near her ankle, like it might be broken. Jeremy knelt by Melanie's side, gently trying to revive her. He had no luck.

Courtney, Reyna, and Jeremy got Harris out of the vehicle last. They weren't very graceful about it. Harris was tall and athletic, kind of a jock, so his body seemed impossibly heavy. They struggled to get him out by yanking on his muscular arms.

Partway through the procedure, he began to wake up. He was confused, and started flailing around. Courtney let go of his arm in surprise and dodged a wild blow, as did Reyna.

"It's me, it's us!" Jeremy yelled at him. "Quit fighting!" Harris's eyes slowly came into focus and he calmed down.

A few minutes later, he was up and talking outside the

SUV. He had a gash across his forehead and one eye was already swollen shut. It was the first time Courtney had seen a person in real life look that bad, like a boxer after losing a fight. She knew it had to hurt.

"Well, this really fucking sucks," he muttered as he stood hunched over with his hands in his pockets. He moved over to Melanie on shaky legs and sat down. He cradled her head in his lap. "C'mon, wake up, sweetie," he said. "Mel, wake up." Like the others, including herself, Courtney noticed he seemed to be in a moderate state of confusion.

Jeremy asked, "Is she breathing okay?" and Harris nodded yes.

Courtney and Reyna got jackets, hats, and gloves out of the car for everyone, as well as any other warm clothes they could find. Then the four of them sat in the snow in a tight circle around Melanie, sheltering next to the SUV in the swath of land it had cleared.

Courtney gazed around at the battered group of survivors, bathed by the light of the full moon. She was so cold she could barely feel her toes or the tips of her fingers anymore, even with extra socks and gloves on. What the hell are we going to do now? she wondered.

"Okay, cell phones," Reyna said. "Who's got one? Mine's still in the car somewhere." Courtney was surprised she hadn't thought of calling for help already and realized she must still be completely out of it. The cold and the trauma of the accident made it hard to concentrate.

"Our phones won't work out here," Jeremy replied glumly. "No grid. We're in the boonies."

"We have to try," Reyna insisted. "It's crazy not to."

"I did already. Right after we wrecked." Jeremy took out his phone and tossed it to Reyna. "You try." Reyna started fumbling to dial with her gloves still on.

Harris had also taken out his cell phone from his pocket and was trying to make it work. Courtney searched aimlessly for hers, but it was gone somewhere. She realized it had probably been thrown out of the SUV, just like she'd been.

The weight of the horror was beginning to sink in. She knew she could have been killed, or paralyzed, or a million other awful things. And she knew they weren't safe yet. The deep snow that had saved her from dying in the accident might now keep all of them prisoners here.

Courtney felt the hairs on her neck prickle with true fear, as Reyna and Harris tried in vain to call for help. None of them had thought the weather would close in like this. A blizzard had been forecast for later in the week, but it had obviously arrived much earlier.

What if no one finds us? Courtney wondered. The road had been completely deserted for at least an hour before the accident. She didn't know what the right protocol for being in an emergency was, because bad things of this magnitude were only supposed to happen to other people.

The agitation made her stand up. "We have to stay

warm until help gets here," she blurted out. "Make a fire. Right?"

Harris looked up at her from his cell phone. "With what? What can we burn? Everything's wet."

"I don't know." She wasn't sure what to say. "There has to be something." She looked at Reyna. Reyna was usually the decisive one, the one with all the ideas who wasn't afraid to speak her mind. In fact, sometimes Courtney had to work hard so that she didn't get lost in her friend's shadow.

Reyna stood up and gave the cell phone back to Jeremy. "Courtney's right. It's too cold to wait here long without a fire." She looked at the ruined SUV. "Maybe we can get the engine back on for heat."

Jeremy shook his head. "Doubt it. That thing is fucked."

Courtney noted that Jeremy didn't sound quite like himself. He was usually dynamic and enthusiastic, but now he sounded dour and old. The accident had made him draw inward somehow. Courtney wondered if she seemed equally strange, or different, to the others.

"We need to get help soon, especially for Melanie," she said. She glanced over at the girl, who was still lying there motionless. Harris had given up on his cell phone and was tending to her. "We don't know what's wrong with her, and I'm really worried."

Reyna nodded. "Me too. If we can't call anyone, a couple of us will have to climb back up to the road and try to flag someone down," she said. "They can take us to the hospital."

"What if the road's blocked and there aren't any cars?" Harris asked Reyna, without looking up from Melanie. "I haven't seen many since Pagosa Springs."

"Maybe they'll clear the road. Maybe they'll send a snowplow. There has to be some way out of here."

Jeremy spoke up. "Unless . . . unless they've totally closed the road down for the storm. It could be closed for a week this time of year."

Reyna looked annoyed. "Geez, guys. Don't be so optimistic. What other choice do we have? Just sitting here?"

Courtney interrupted before Reyna and Jeremy could get into an argument. She knew that was the last thing anyone needed.

"Let's try the SUV first," she said. "If we can get the engine on, we can continue the debate in there." Her words still sounded like they had a weird echo. Harris wiped a hand across Melanie's face to keep it clear of falling snow.

"Okay, the Explorer," Reyna said. "Jeremy, you got the keys?"

"They're still in the ignition."

"I'll go try it, then."

"I can help—" Jeremy said, but Reyna cut him off.

"No, you might not fit."

Reyna sounded assertive as usual, which Courtney thought was a good thing. Occasionally that trait of Reyna's—wanting to boss people around—drove her crazy, but here it looked like it would be an asset.

18

As Courtney and the others waited, Reyna clambered back inside the SUV and made her way up to the front, climbing between the squashed roof and the seats. Courtney listened to the sounds of the engine clicking and trying to turn over, but despite Reyna's efforts, it never caught. A minute or two later she crawled out of the SUV and back to their huddled circle, where Courtney and the others waited in various degrees of despair and pain.

"It's dead," Reyna said, "and the key's jammed in the ignition. I couldn't even pull it out." She looked over at Courtney as if seeking advice.

"Then let's make a fire," Courtney volunteered, thinking they had to keep Melanie warm. "Once the fire's started, we can split up and some of us can go for the road." The idea of splitting up the group frightened Courtney, but she knew it was the smartest thing to do. It would increase their chances of getting rescued quickly.

"What a disaster," Jeremy murmured, putting his head in his hands. "No one's going to help us."

"It could be worse. A lot worse." Reyna didn't say the unspoken, that one of them, or more, could have died in the wreck.

Of course they didn't know what was wrong with Melanie yet, Courtney thought, so maybe it was premature to think that way. *What if Melanie's dying right now?*

Courtney spoke so she wouldn't have to face such awful things. The words came out in an ungainly, desperate rush: "With a fire and all our ski clothes, we'll be able to stay warm for a while. It'll suck, but even if no one finds us tonight, we can make it through till morning. When the sun comes up we can start walking if we have to."

"Walk where?" Jeremy muttered, but Reyna was nodding, as though this seemed like a plan she could get behind.

Reyna checked her watch. "It's two a.m. Less than five hours until sunrise. It won't be so bad with a fire."

Courtney brushed snow from her hair. "Of course that's worst-case scenario. Let's hope it doesn't come to that."

Harris looked up. "If it does, we'll need to find stuff to burn." He dug a chrome cigarette lighter out of the pocket of his jeans. "I guess this is when it pays to smoke." He flicked the flint, and a tiny yellow flame flared up for a second, like a little beacon of hope.

Courtney thought it was surreal to see the lighter in his hand. She remembered the last time she'd seen him hold it up. It had been less than twenty-four hours ago, in the condo they'd shared at the ski lodge. He'd been demonstrating how to open a beer bottle with it, a trick Courtney had never seen before.

We were having fun then, she thought. Fun now seemed like an alien concept. It was staggering to think how the trajectory of their lives had changed so drastically in less than a day.

"I've read about what people do when stuff like this happens," Reyna said. "It's easy to start a fire, and lots of things are flammable, you'd be surprised. People even burn their money if they get desperate enough."

"We're not that desperate," Harris said. "Are we?" He wiped some snot away from his nose with the back of his gloved hand.

"There're a couple magazines and newspapers in the car," Courtney said, suddenly remembering. "If they're still there, that is. I was reading them earlier. And there're some pillows too."

"Good. We can start with those." Reyna turned to head back into the SUV.

Courtney stood up to follow her. Seeing the flame of the lighter had made her hungry for warmth. And she also felt bad that Reyna was having to do everything herself. Courtney was a little surprised that Jeremy was being so quiet. Harris, she could understand. If she were in Melanie's position, she'd want her boyfriend to spend all his energy looking after her too. Of course she was single now—since she'd broken up with her boyfriend, Chris, back in October—so the whole idea was sadly hypothetical.

Courtney and Reyna fished the magazines and pillows out of the SUV, along with a roll of paper towels they found. They put everything on top of a suitcase and placed it on the snow in the clearing near Melanie. It looked like a woefully small amount of fuel for a fire.

"So we just light it or what?" Courtney asked. She knew they should gather some tree branches, but she figured the wood would be too damp to burn. Everything was buried under snow. "Don't we need lighter fluid for the pillows?"

Jeremy stood up, grimacing. "No, I can do it. I was in the Cub Scouts when I was a kid."

Harris suddenly smiled despite himself. "For real?"

"My parents made me join. But I never thought any of the crap I learned would come in useful."

Harris tossed Jeremy the lighter, and he got the fire started after only a few tries. The pillows emitted a harsh chemical smell, but at least they caught easily. It didn't look like the kind of fire that would burn for very long, however, or give out much heat. The flames were thin and yellow. Still, they put their hands out over it, trying to warm their fingers.

Courtney couldn't feel her toes and was afraid she was getting frostbite already. She didn't say anything about it, though. She felt like it might jinx her to bring it up. Besides, she was usually the kind of person who preferred to keep her worries inside, rather than spill her thoughts out into the open. Courtney knew some people found her attitude weird, but she didn't care.

Are we fucking up here? Courtney wondered as she watched the flames. There was a knot in her stomach that felt like dread. She had the feeling there were things they could be doing, important things, that might help them get to safety. But Courtney didn't have any survival-type experience, and neither did her friends. The extent of their knowledge was Jeremy's Cub Scout years.

"We'll have to find more stuff to keep this fire going," Reyna said. From the look in her eyes, Courtney could tell she didn't know what to do either.

Courtney pulled her scarf up to her nose so it covered more of her face. It offered little protection against the cold. "We should go up to the road now."

"Agreed," Reyna said. "And if we don't see any cars, maybe we could walk up it a ways. Try to find a house or a rest stop, or something. It's cold, but it's not that cold. Maybe twenty-five degrees?" It sounded like a wild guess. "Warm for January. It's not like we'd die."

Courtney could sense the mix of optimism and desperation in her friend's voice. She knew Reyna was faking her confident tone.

"I can't leave Melanie," Harris said. "Otherwise, I'd be up for it."

"Makes sense. Courtney and I will go together."

"Mel would be pissed as hell if she woke up and I wasn't here," Harris elaborated, his voice suddenly cracking slightly. For a brief flicker of an instant Courtney felt jealous of Melanie. It was idiotic and kind of sick, she knew, because Melanie was unconscious and her leg was probably broken. But Courtney was jealous that the girl had someone who cared about her so much. If it were her still passed out on the snow, would anyone care like that? Reyna would, but that was no substitute for a boyfriend.

Jeremy raised his head to look at Courtney and Reyna. "I'll go with you."

"Why? Your side is hurting you, it's obvious. Even though you're trying to pretend you're okay."

Jeremy seemed surprised that Reyna had noticed. "It can't just be two girls. Something might happen to you. Either me or Harris needs to go too, and he said he wants to stay."

"We don't need to argue gender politics right now," Reyna said tiredly. "We don't need to argue about anything. What we need to do is go get help."

Jeremy struggled forward, clutching his side like an old man. "The three of us can go," he insisted.

Harris didn't look too pleased with the idea. "But that means it's just me and Melanie left behind. How am I supposed to look after her and keep the fire going?" He looked at Jeremy. "Dude, just stay here with me. The girls will be fine. They're tough."

"You got that right," Reyna replied.

Courtney played through all the combinations in her mind. If Harris was determined to stay with his girlfriend, which he was, and Jeremy was clearly more hurt than he was letting on, it made the most sense for her and Reyna to walk up the road alone. The more time they wasted talking, the worse it would be for them.

"Jer, just stay here," she said to him, trading on the fact they'd been friends for so long, and that sometimes he actually listened to her. "Please. We'll just walk a little bit and see if we can flag down a car. Even though it's late, someone might be on the road. If not, we'll come right back. You can go through the stuff in the meantime—find out if we have any food or anything to drink."

Jeremy wavered, but then finally capitulated. "Okay. But just be careful out there."

To Courtney, his words sounded like a line from a bad TV show, but she appreciated the sentiment.

"Sure thing," Reyna told him. Then she tried to make a joke: "Hey, if we're not back in an hour, call the police." No one laughed, so she turned to Courtney. "Ready, girl?"

Courtney nodded, pulling her scarf tighter, trying to keep out the icy wind. "Let's do it."

III

Courtney and Reyna slowly made it out of the forest and back up the embankment to the long, forbidding road. They moved deliberately and with great caution through the thick snow. Courtney felt like she was wading through water. It was still snowing a little, and grains of ice kept sticking to her eyelashes as she walked.

When they reached the barren road, they paused and looked up and down it. The tracks left by the SUV and the debris from the accident were partially covered with snow. There was no indication that any other vehicles had passed them. The highway was desolate in both directions.

There was also no sign of the deer they had hit, Courtney noted. Maybe its body was down the embankment somewhere, or maybe it had lived and limped away.

Out on the exposed road, the wind was much worse. It seemed to cut through Courtney's layers of clothes, slicing at her skin. Any area that wasn't completely covered, like her cheeks and nose, was either raw or numb.

Courtney glanced over at Reyna, who had taken something out of her pocket. It took Courtney a moment to figure out what it was.

"Lip balm," Reyna said, when she noticed that Courtney was watching her. "Don't want to get chapped."

Courtney was oddly fascinated by how her friend seemed to be dealing with this horrific new environment. She supposed she was comforted by the way Reyna was acting like everything was okay, but she was also a little thrown by it. What do chapped lips matter at this point? Courtney wondered. Yet Reyna always seemed this self-assured, even when it was a pretense.

"Ready to start walking?" Reyna asked when she'd finished applying the balm.

"I guess we have to be. Which way?"

Reyna thought for a moment. "North, the way we were headed. I don't remember passing any houses, so there's no point going back. Besides, there's just something more reassuring about going forward."

Courtney wasn't sure she agreed, but she didn't feel like arguing. She guessed it didn't matter much which direction they chose.

As they started walking, Courtney saw something

sticking up at an angle from the snow ahead of them. It was one of their skis, or what was left of it. She made a mental note to pick it up on the way back, in case they could use it somehow.

Courtney glanced up at the sky. It was layered with white clouds, illuminated from behind by the moon. Because of the clouds and the snow, the light was much brighter than normal for nighttime. Everything seemed to have a strange reflective glow to it, a weird sort of phosphorescence that created a feeling like being underwater.

"Hey look!" Reyna said, finding something else in the snow. She was a few steps ahead of Courtney. Courtney caught up to her just as Reyna picked up the item. "A book."

Courtney leaned over to look as Reyna brushed the snow and ice off the leather-bound, pocket-size volume. Courtney recognized it right away, even before Reyna opened it. "It's Jeremy's," Courtney said. "It's his journal."

Reyna looked at her, surprised. "Jeremy? Are you serious? I didn't know guys kept journals."

"I've seen him writing in it sometimes." Courtney wasn't sure she was supposed to have seen him, because Jeremy was fairly covert about it. Yet she'd noticed because she kept a journal too, since she was twelve, and wanted to be a writer one day. More than once she'd wondered what was in Jeremy's journal, and if she'd been inscribed in its pages somewhere.

This was because since her breakup with Chris,

Courtney had nursed a sporadic crush on Jeremy, not that anyone had noticed. She hadn't shared it with Reyna because it embarrassed her. Sometimes Jeremy seemed attractive, and other times not.

"A journal. Who would have thought," Reyna muttered. "But I guess it makes sense. Jeremy's so frigging emo."

"Nothing wrong with that."

"Oh yeah, I forgot you don't mind skinny boys." Reyna frowned. "Or vegetarians. I could never date a guy who eats less than I do."

Courtney was inwardly amused for a second, because she guessed that if Reyna ever chose to read the journal, she might learn something surprising. Courtney knew something that Reyna didn't, something that had been confided to her after a drunken party in strictest confidence: Jeremy had a crush on Reyna. He had, however, been too shy to do anything about it yet. Courtney was embarrassed by the whole thing, because it seemed like some cheesy love triangle straight out of a daytime soap.

Reyna tucked the journal under her arm. "I bet he'll be glad we rescued this. He should just keep a blog like the rest of us so his writing doesn't get lost."

"Maybe he doesn't want anyone else reading it."

"Then what's the point of writing?" Reyna paused. "I wonder what other stuff is out here." She started looking around as though she wanted to go digging in the snow for treasure, like a beachcomber with a metal detector.

"We don't have time for a scavenger hunt," Courtney told her, unnerved that Reyna was acting so blasé about their situation. "Let's get moving, okay?"

Grudgingly, Reyna acquiesced, putting Jeremy's journal into her jacket pocket. Soon they were walking again, making slow but steady progress up the road. Courtney had long since given up on the idea that a car might drive by, because the road looked completely impassable, even by Colorado standards. But she still clung to the idea that perhaps a snowplow would come to clear it, even if she knew it was doubtful.

They walked for about twenty minutes, mostly without talking, because it took so much effort to keep moving. The air felt impossibly clean, as though the blizzard had removed all the impurities from it. Yet the freezing temperatures meant that it burned Courtney's nose and throat with each breath that she sucked in. Her legs ached too. The initial shock of the accident had worn off, and the pain was getting worse, but she pushed herself forward. She didn't want to let herself or her friends down. They were depending on her, especially Melanie.

"God, I'm hungry," Reyna murmured at one point, and Courtney could only agree mutely. She'd been fantasizing about warm comfort food and coffee since they began their trek through the wilderness.

The landscape was serene but implacable in its harshness. There were no signs of life, not even animals. It was just a velvety blanket of snow in all directions, smothering everything with its freezing touch. The

31

green of the trees had been erased by white. Courtney kept wondering about the deer that had run into the road. She didn't know why it mattered, but she hoped it had escaped injury—even if it had caused all their misery.

Reyna finally stopped moving, and Courtney took it as her cue to do the same. She was out of breath, panting, and felt cold sweat under her layers of clothes. She could hear Reyna struggling for breath too.

"See that?" Reyna asked, pointing up ahead. Her arm was shaking a little from fatigue. "I think it's a light."

Courtney struggled to see. The reflections and general weirdness of the snow-covered landscape made it hard to tell. She thought maybe she saw a flickering orange glow coming from the left-hand side of the road in the distance, but she knew it could be an illusion.

"Something's up there." Reyna sounded certain. "It might be a house. Maybe one of those weigh stations for trucks or something."

"That's a long way from here," Courtney said, still trying to figure out what they were looking at. "I don't know if we should risk it. Maybe we should turn back." She was longing for even the meager heat from their little fire. "We can come back out later."

"We can't turn back now," Reyna said. She inhaled deeply, and then exhaled, releasing a visible plume of breath. "I know it sucks, but we have to keep going and get to the light."

Courtney knew Reyna was probably right. If it was a

house, then they could get help, and be out of this nightmare within the hour. But Courtney would have to find a way to motivate her leaden arms and legs into action. It occurred to her to say she just wanted to sit and rest in the snow while Reyna walked up to the light. But that seemed particularly lame, and the idea of being alone on the road frankly terrified her.

"Okay," Courtney said with a sigh. "But if nothing's there, then we go back."

Reyna nodded her agreement. "Deal." They began to walk slowly again.

It took another twenty minutes before they reached the source of the orange light, although Courtney saw what it was before they got there. It was a strange, squat building, made of gray cinder block, just to the left of the road. Snowdrifts nearly covered one side of it so that it merged into the landscape. There was a single orange light hanging above the front door, and it cast odd shadows across the snow.

Reyna started rejoicing as soon as they saw the building. "I knew it!" Reyna said, as she began moving faster. "C'mon, it's a house! Let's go!" But Courtney knew that just because there was a light, didn't mean there would be people.

When the two of them got there, they stood in the road, panting in the snow. Other than the lone lightbulb, the place looked deserted.

"It's dark in there," Courtney said, surveying the building. The windows stared out blankly, like dead eyes. She noticed all the windows had metal security bars on them, which meant they wouldn't be able to break inside to call for help.

Although the building seemed abandoned, Reyna was undeterred. "That doesn't mean anything. Let's go knock."

She and Courtney headed up the short driveway to the front door. The snow was thicker here, and it was blowing off the roof of the building, spraying down their necks.

"What is this place, anyway?" Courtney asked.

"I don't—" Reyna began, but then she stopped. "Wait, here's a sign." There was a metal plaque on the wall next to the front door. " 'Maitland County Highway Services,' " she read, then added, "Whatever the hell that means . . ."

She searched for a doorbell as Courtney came up behind her, but there wasn't one, so they started banging on the front door and calling for help. Courtney knew their effort was probably in vain. *There's no one here,* she thought. *This is just some glorified storage shed for highway equipment.* Finally she stopped and said, "Rey, this isn't working."

Reyna reluctantly stopped pounding on the door. "I can't believe no one's here," she grumbled, dejected. "Why'd they leave a light on?"

"It's probably automatic. Look, we should just go back—"

Reyna cut her off: "Not yet. We have to go around the

34

building, see if there's another way inside. I know they have a phone in there. I just know it."

"I think all the windows have bars on them."

"We'll be quick."

Courtney and Reyna trudged around the circumference of the small building but soon discovered there really was no way in. The building was a dead end.

They walked back around to the front door. Courtney noticed it had started snowing harder again, on top of everything else. She kept stamping her feet and flexing her toes to try to get blood circulating through them. She wondered if Reyna felt as cold as she did.

"What do we do now?" Reyna asked, sounding depressed.

Courtney hoped it wasn't meant as a rhetorical question, because she was eager to answer it. She burst in and said, "We go back to the SUV." She was missing the safety of the group and felt exposed out by the desolate building.

Reyna frowned and said, "So you want to give up?"

Courtney knew Reyna wanted to press onward, to be the one who somehow saved the group. But out here Courtney refused to be subject to her friend's whims, because their lives potentially were at stake.

"Listen, I'm scared and I'm cold," she said. "When the sun comes up and it's warmer, and we can see better, we'll come back out here and try again. There aren't any cars—the road's obviously impassable. And this doesn't look like the kind of road that's going to have any houses on it, anyway. It's kind of crazy to keep walking around in this much snow."

"I'm not being crazy," Reyna retorted. "I'm just trying to help us. Don't get pissy."

Courtney fought the urge to roll her eyes. Although she and Reyna were as close as sisters, that also meant they sometimes squabbled like sisters. Courtney rubbed her aching head. "I'm far from pissy. Many leagues from pissy, in fact. But can we just be rational for a moment?" She paused as Reyna sulked. "I'm so tired I feel like I'm going to pass out," Courtney continued. "We need to get back to the others and the fire, and try to get ourselves warm. They're probably wondering what happened to us. I just can't stand being out here anymore. My whole body hurts after the accident, doesn't yours?" Snow got in her eyes again and she wiped it away. "Aren't you tired?"

"Maybe Jeremy should have come with us after all," Reyna said finally.

The words hurt Courtney's feelings. "Now who's being pissy?" she snapped back. "Jeremy's injured, and no one else would go with you, so too bad. You're stuck with me."

For a brief second she thought Reyna was going to argue with her, but then she realized that Reyna wasn't listening at all. In fact, she wasn't even looking at Courtney. She was peering through the curtains of gently falling snow at something across the road, a little farther up.

Courtney sighed, rubbing her gloved hands together for warmth. "What is it?" she asked, resigned to the fact that Reyna was apparently on her own wavelength.

"I think I see a car," Reyna replied softly.

"What?!" The words surprised Courtney, because she definitely didn't see any vehicles anywhere. The road was completely abandoned, like before.

"Not on the road," Reyna elaborated, as if reading Courtney's mind, "but over there." She pointed. "Off the road in the ditch."

Courtney squinted. All she saw at first were curvy snowdrifts and the ominous shapes of snow-covered branches bending under their weight. But then, as she kept looking, she caught the glint of something shiny and metallic. And as her eyes locked onto it and focused, the faint shape of a white van came into view, half buried in the snow. "Oh my God," Courtney breathed. "You're right. How the hell did you see that?"

"Good eyesight." Reyna wiped her nose on the back of her sleeve. Both her nose and Courtney's were running constantly from the intense cold. "They probably got stranded like us," Reyna said. "We better check it out."

"Yeah, you think?" Courtney asked. The tension between her and Reyna had instantly evaporated. Seeing the car made Courtney feel hopeful again, because maybe there were people huddled inside, just like them. And maybe those people had food, or warmth, or a cell phone that got reception, or any number of things that could help her and Reyna.

The two of them headed directly across the road, in the direction of the waiting van. Courtney's breath was caught in her chest from anticipation of what they might find.

As they neared the van, Courtney noticed that it didn't look like it had been in an accident, which was a good sign. Although parts of it were hidden by the snow, everything looked intact. The van was large, with windows along the side, and it had some sort of black logo or emblem near the back, masked by a snowdrift.

Please let us get some help here, Courtney prayed, as they drew even closer. *We really need it.*

IV

Courtney and Reyna reached the van, stumbling against its frigid hull. Together they cupped their hands around their faces and pressed them to the glass. At first Courtney couldn't make sense of the strange shape she saw slumped across the front seats. Then it all coalesced, and she realized she was looking at the body of a naked man.

Courtney let out a gasp of surprise, and she felt Reyna grab on to her. The man was lying facedown with his head on the passenger seat, so his back was mostly visible. His skin was gray, and he wasn't moving.

Courtney clutched Reyna as she struggled to force the words out: "Is he dead?"

"I think so," her friend whispered back.

Courtney nodded slowly, still not taking her eyes off

the man. She had never seen a dead body before, but there was a stillness to his presence that let her know he probably wasn't alive anymore. Besides, she thought, it was so cold out here. No one could survive without clothes on, even inside a van.

"We have to check," Reyna murmured. She didn't sound too thrilled about the prospect. "Maybe he's just hurt."

"Why is he naked?" Courtney whispered to Reyna. She supposed there could be many reasons, but it was bizarre, and it made her uneasy.

Reyna didn't have an answer. She reached out and took hold of the latch, preparing to open the driver's-side door. Courtney took a step back. She didn't know what to expect. For all they knew, the man was alive and could burst up like a monster in a horror movie.

"Rey?" she warned. "Are you sure about this? Maybe we should leave it alone and come back with the guys."

Reyna paused, her gloved fingers still about to open the door. "We have to find out for sure," she said. "If he's alive and we don't help him now, it could be too late . . ." Then she added, "But part of me really hopes this door is locked."

Before Courtney could say anything else, Reyna tugged on the latch, and Courtney heard a click. The door slowly came open, the bottom part dragging against the snow. Courtney stood there, too afraid to move, as Reyna pulled the door wide, giving them a clear view into the van's interior. There was some kind of mangled divider between the front seats and the back, a wire mesh fence with a huge hole in it, but Courtney's eyes were glued to the man's body in the front.

Definitely dead, Courtney thought, feeling numb—and not from the cold. The body was rigid and impossibly still. There were two strange wounds on his back, large bloody holes, and a pool of dark liquid in the well of the passenger seat. Courtney looked away and noticed there were no keys in the ignition.

"Sir?" Reyna called out into the cold night air that had infiltrated the van. Courtney guessed she could tell the man was dead too. "Uh, hello?"

There was no response. Courtney scrutinized the figure. If the man's body had been elsewhere, she might have believed he was sleeping. He was overweight, with little dark hairs all over his back and his butt, and although his face and head were masked in shadows, she could tell he was balding.

Courtney realized she was holding her breath and she let it out in a slow, soft exhalation. She waited a moment before she said, "Reyna, he's dead. Let's go."

Reyna turned back to look at her. Courtney saw a mixture of fear and curiosity in her eyes, but also a desire to help. "We have to check if he's breathing. What if he's alive, but got hypothermia? It's possible."

Courtney guessed Reyna wasn't quite as freaked out by the body as she was. She knew Reyna wanted to be a doctor, like her father, and had even done community work at the local hospital. So seeing dead bodies might be nothing new to her, Courtney thought. *But it sure as hell is for me.*

"Check him out, then," Courtney said. "There's no way I'm touching him. I'm standing right here." She wanted to defend her right to be scared.

Reyna stepped forward and removed one of her gloves. "I'm going to try feeling for a pulse."

"Just do it fast."

"I should be able to get one from his ankle." Reyna reached out tentatively to touch the man's foot. Courtney saw there were calluses on it, like he did a lot of walking in uncomfortable shoes. Reyna's hand moved closer to the foot, until the tips of her fingers grazed his skin. A second after contact, she recoiled quickly, as though his flesh had burned her. "He's cold!" she said. "Like ice."

"I guess that answers your question," Courtney managed. She looked away from the body again because she was starting to feel sick. She noticed that Reyna was wiping her hand on the leg of her jeans.

"Ugh," Reyna said. "It was like touching prime rib in a meat locker."

Courtney shuddered and tried not to think about that image too much.

"And look—" Reyna gestured with her ungloved hand. "No breath."

It was true, Courtney noted. In the cold air, she and Reyna had constant puffs of smoke coming from their mouths whenever they talked. But it didn't look like the man was breathing at all.

"What do you think killed him?"

"Don't know."

Something attached to the dashboard caught Courtney's eye. "I think that's a CB radio," she said. "We could call for help."

Reyna reached back in, over the body, and fiddled with the knobs, but nothing happened. Courtney waited next to her in the cold, shivering.

Reyna finally said, "It's as dead as the driver." She pulled her glove back on. After touching the body, some of her confidence seemed to have slipped away. She now looked as eager as Courtney to leave the van behind and get back to their friends. "We'll tell everyone what we found."

Courtney turned away from the van, and the corpse within it. As she stepped back, she noticed the emblem painted on the side again. It was near the back, mostly hidden by the snow. She didn't know what compelled her to do it, but she took a couple deep steps over to it and wiped away some of the snow. Her efforts revealed a single word: *Maitland.* Courtney supposed that made sense, given they were apparently in Maitland County. She thought maybe the van had something to do with the locked building across the street.

Reyna saw what she was doing and said, "Yeah, good idea." The words encouraged Courtney to keep going.

She dug out some more snow to uncover the other words hidden in the circular emblem. It only took a few more swipes until Courtney, with a sudden jolt, realized exactly what the words said, and what the van was.

"Oh God . . ." she said as she stumbled backward a step. She didn't even need to say anything further, because Reyna understood at once.

" 'Maitland County Correctional Facility,' " Reyna read out loud. She looked over at Courtney. "It's a prison van." For the first time, Courtney detected a note of genuine fear in Reyna's voice. "What's it doing out here?"

Courtney felt anxiety rising up inside her, making her chest feel tight, but she pushed the sensation back down. "We have to get out of this place, Rey." She swallowed, her face feeling stiff from the cold. "Something bad happened here."

Reyna was looking away from her, past her, as though scanning the snow-covered landscape. "The dead man. He was probably one of the guards." She paused. "And whoever did this, they're probably out here somewhere."

Courtney felt her arms prickling with goose bumps. "We're not safe on the road."

Reyna turned back to look at her. Courtney could tell her friend was feeling very scared now. That only made her feel worse, because Reyna was supposed to be the brave one. "I think—" Reyna began, "—that whoever was being transported in this van killed the guard and took off."

Courtney nodded. Talking about it made her fear increase, although she knew they had to face the reality of their situation. "They could still be nearby. We don't know how many there are." Her mouth felt dry.

"It doesn't matter. There could be one person, or there could be more." Reyna paused. "Whatever they were in prison for must have been pretty bad if they were desperate enough to murder someone to escape."

Courtney couldn't stop a parade of violent images from rushing through her mind. The van was large enough to hold maybe ten convicts at most, which meant there might be that many out there with them in the blizzard. *Thieves. Murderers. Rapists.* She didn't want to think about what would happen if she and Reyna crossed paths with any of these men, or if the men found Jeremy, Harris, and Melanie.

Courtney watched the forest, listening closely. Other than the noise of branches creaking under the weight of the snow, there were no ominous sounds, and she saw no signs of footprints. "Let's head back. We'll have to stick together from now on."

"No kidding."

Courtney wrapped her scarf tighter around her neck again, and then she and Reyna began their long journey back to the ruined SUV. They moved as swiftly as they could, given the circumstances. The depth of the snow made it impossible to run, but they lugged themselves along, holding on to each other for balance every now and then.

Courtney was having difficulty taking stock of her emotions. She couldn't think of the dead body without feeling sick and scared, although she had to admit she felt a morbid curiosity about it. How had the man been killed? Who had done it?

Even more important questions threatened to overwhelm her as she traversed the snowdrifts alongside Reyna. If the killer, or killers, were still out there, would they come after her and her friends? She hoped the killers had moved on, as there was clearly no incentive for them to hang around in a blizzard. However, she also knew there was no place for them to go. It was likely they were just as stranded as she and the others were.

The snow continued to fall in lush white sheets that would have been beautiful under other conditions. But here, the snow was terrifying and blinding. It had already smoothed over the tracks they'd made on their journey, and Courtney was worried they'd miss the crash site and walk right past the SUV.

"Wait—" she heard Reyna hiss in her ear, breaking her train of thought.

Courtney slowed and came to a stop, her legs wedged in the snow, propping her upright. "What?"

"I think I heard something. . . ."

The two of them stood there, disoriented and afraid. Courtney didn't hear anything, but she trusted Reyna and the girl's hyperacute senses. They stood as still as rocks. After a moment, Courtney dared to whisper, "What kind of sound?"

"I don't know."

"A person?"

"Maybe. Could have been an animal."

"Let's keep walking," Courtney said. She didn't want to stand around and wait for something scary to come out of the forest and find them.

But then Courtney heard the sound too. It did not, thankfully, sound like a person to her. It was a strange, distant baying sound, like the wail of a coyote. There was a mournful quality to it, but a dangerous, edgy one too. Courtney didn't know exactly what sort of animal was out there in the cold with them, and she wasn't eager to find out.

"I hear it," Courtney said. She took a step back down the road, and then another. She worried if she didn't take action, Reyna might stand there longer, trying to analyze the sound in greater detail. "Reyna, c'mon. I don't want us to get killed."

"What do you think it is?"

"Nothing we want to meet, so let's keep moving."

"Okay, okay," Reyna said. She followed after Courtney nervously. Soon the eerie sound was fading behind them in the distance.

During their entire return trip to the SUV, no other cars passed them. This road definitely seems closed for the storm, Courtney thought. Which meant they were stuck, until their parents figured out they were missing, or the road was reopened when the blizzard passed. She knew that either of those things might take a very long time. They were not on a major road, so it wouldn't be a high priority for it to get cleared. And Courtney's parents weren't super strict about curfew since she'd turned sixteen, so they were used to her getting home late. They wouldn't start worrying until morning at the earliest. She could only hope someone else's parents would call the police tonight.

Courtney was overcome with the greatest desire she'd ever known just to get warm and to rest in a safe place. Her arms and legs felt weighted down, and her head was heavy. She hoped that when they got back, Melanie would be awake, and not too badly hurt. She knew they'd need all the energy they could muster to protect themselves.

People have probably died in situations a lot less serious than this one, she told herself. The thought didn't give her any solace, but it did motivate her to try to be careful and not make any stupid mistakes.

Courtney looked up ahead and saw the broken ski sticking up from the road. "We're almost there," she said to Reyna, pointing.

Reyna followed her gaze and nodded. She and Courtney continued down the road, heading toward the ditch and the hole in the forest. They picked up the ski on their way. Neither of them knew what they would find at the SUV, or what kind of shape their friends would be in. Courtney hoped for the best, but feared the worst.

V

When Courtney and Reyna got back to the SUV, they found Jeremy tending to the fire with a stick. Embers and smoke were coming off it, and the smell of burning wood was a comforting reminder of her fireplace back home. Courtney felt a rush of relief. She'd been inexplicably afraid that they'd get back and find no one there.

Courtney saw that Melanie was awake too, groggily sitting up, propped against one of their surviving suitcases. Harris was sitting next to her, and they were sharing a half-empty bottle of orange Gatorade that must have been salvaged from the SUV.

All three of them looked toward Courtney and Reyna as the two of them stumbled into the clearing. Courtney couldn't wait to get to the fire and warm her feet and hands. She saw a stockpile near the fire of five other small bottles of Gatorade, plus some sodas, energy bars, and a couple bags of potato chips. There were also two backpacks, and next to them, a large metal hatchet with a wooden handle. The hatchet belonged to Jeremy's dad, and they had been using it to chop wood at the condo in Pagosa Springs.

Jeremy waded quickly in their direction, giving both of them hugs. But Courtney noticed he couldn't keep the look of disappointment from his face. Clearly he'd hoped they would return with people who could rescue them.

"Did you find anything?" he asked, as he led Courtney and Reyna over to the fire. "You were gone so long."

"Yeah, long time no see," Harris said. Melanie waved weakly at them. There was a dazed look in her eyes, like she wasn't all the way awake yet. Courtney put down the ski and went over and hugged her.

Courtney knew neither she nor Reyna wanted to explain to everyone what they'd found out there in the snow. She wasn't even sure where to begin. The fire and the companionship of the others created the illusion of safety for the moment, but anything she'd say would wreck it.

"You guys look like you saw a ghost or something," Jeremy added, as Reyna and Courtney grabbed bottles of Gatorade.

Reyna spoke up first. "We did, kind of." She sat down close to the fire and took off her wet gloves as Courtney did the same.

"What do you mean?" Harris asked. "Were there any cars out there? Did you get help?"

Courtney thought it was pretty obvious that they hadn't, but she just shook her head.

"Shit," Harris muttered. "The road's closed, isn't it?"

"It looks that way," Courtney replied, thinking they had far worse problems on their hands than the road.

Reyna looked around at the group. "Courtney and I have some bad news. We did find a car, only it wasn't running . . ." Her words trailed away.

Harris frowned, looking puzzled. "Another wreck?"

Reyna shook her head. "Not exactly. I don't want to freak everyone out, but the car was stuck, and the driver was dead. He'd been killed." Blank faces greeted her pronouncement; no one wanted to believe her.

"It was some kind of prison van," Courtney added, "and it looked like people had escaped from it. I think we might be in danger."

A long silence greeted her words, punctuated only by the crackling and popping sounds of damp wood in the flames.

"Jesus," Jeremy finally said. "Are you sure? I mean, the guy was really dead?"

Courtney nodded slowly. Everyone kept looking at her so she said, "He was naked, too. Someone had taken his clothes."

Melanie looked very frightened and burrowed closer into Harris, under his arm.

"That's crazy," Harris said as he stroked his girlfriend's

hair. "What would a prison van be doing way out here?"

"Who knows?" Reyna asked. "I mean, what are we doing here, right? We didn't plan to take this route, or to get stuck. It just happened."

Courtney could hear the fear in their voices, and it made her heart beat faster. She felt an urge to share everything with them. "We heard some weird sounds too, nearby in the forest. Like an animal was out there. But I guess it could have been a person."

"Great," Jeremy muttered. "Fucking great." He rubbed his side with one hand in an unconscious gesture, as though it had started hurting him again. "So we think some deranged killer might be out here with us?"

"Maybe more than one," Reyna replied. "We need to put out the fire so it doesn't give our position away. If someone, or something, is out there, then we can't let them find us."

Melanie looked up at the group. Her eyes were soft and wounded-looking, and when she spoke, her voice sounded frail. "Don't take the fire away." They were the first words Courtney had heard her say since waking up.

"Yeah," Harris agreed. "How are we going to stay warm?"

"It's better to take our chances with the weather than get killed by some escaped convict," Reyna told him.

"Not if we die from hypothermia first."

"No, Reyna's right," Jeremy said. He picked at some dried blood on the side of his face. "We need to kill the fire and hole up in the SUV. We can barricade ourselves inside, put on all the clothes we have, and try to stay warm that way."

Courtney didn't like the idea of going back into the SUV, but she knew it was probably a good idea. It would hold their body heat somewhat, and they could make it through the rest of the night. She knew it couldn't be more than three or four hours until the sun came up.

"I think that's a stupid idea, dude," Harris was muttering.

To try to resolve the discussion, Courtney said, "The SUV is the perfect place to hide. In fact, it's the only place."

Harris didn't seem convinced, but now he was outnumbered. Grudgingly, he said: "Maybe." Melanie didn't say anything. Courtney wished she knew the two of them better so she could tell what they were thinking.

"So we hide in the SUV until sunrise," she said. "What then?"

"We get rescued," Reyna replied. "Helicopters will be out looking for us, I'm sure." Courtney thought she sounded a little too confident, like she was still putting on an act for the others.

What if we don't get rescued? she wanted to ask, but didn't. *What if the prisoners come in the night and find us?* But as was frequently the case, it was nicer to believe in a positive scenario than question it.

Harris clearly didn't share that opinion. "What happens if it keeps snowing?" he asked. "What if no one comes tomorrow, and we have to hike all the way out of here ourselves? There's no way Melanie can do it 'cause she's hurt, and we can't leave her. What if we're stuck?"

"This blizzard can't go on forever," Reyna said, as Jeremy nodded somberly. "It'll break sometime. Even if it takes longer than a day. Then the road will open up and the helicopters and snowplows will come. We'll be back in Denver within forty-eight hours, tops."

"We don't have much food," Harris pointed out, sounding increasingly agitated. "And there are murdering convicts out there—" He broke off. "You make it sound so easy."

Reyna wasn't fazed. "We can't control the convicts, and we can't control the weather. All we can control is ourselves. If we stay calm and keep warm, we'll survive just fine until someone finds us. And if no one comes, once the sun's up, some of us will try to get help again." She paused, playing with the ski pass stuck to the zipper of her jacket. "We're not in the Arctic Circle, for God's sake. We're in Maitland, Colorado. We're only three hours from home. Just keep your shit together. Please."

Harris was about to say something more, but Reyna turned away from him, snubbing him. Courtney saw her take something out of her jacket pocket and realized it was Jeremy's journal.

"Here," Reyna said, holding it out to Jeremy. "Take it."

Jeremy looked startled. Courtney guessed he hadn't known it was missing yet. "Thanks," he said, embarrassed. He took it quickly and stuffed it into the pocket of his own jacket.

"So let's put out this fire," Reyna said. "Because I don't want us to end up like that guy in the prison van."

A half hour later, the fire was out, and all five of them had crammed themselves into the SUV. They'd shoved suit-cases, clothes, and other items into the broken windows to seal up the inside and keep in the warmth generated by their bodies. Without the fire, it was ice-cold and barely tolerable. The crushed roof was so low that it created a disorienting effect and didn't give them much headroom. They'd discovered that the dome light inside still worked, albeit faintly, but they kept it off for fear of being seen.

Jeremy and Harris had managed to lower the back-seat, so that the area behind the driver and passenger seats was just one large, open space for them to huddle in. Melanie was stretching her injured leg out in the far back, next to Harris, while Jeremy and Reyna were closer to the front.

Courtney, however, was up in the driver's seat, crammed near the windshield. It was cracked but unbro-ken, so she could stare out into the moonlit snow at the trees. The moon made everything look washed-out and monochromatic. She had taken the front seat because she'd volunteered to keep watch first. She knew there was no way she'd fall asleep soon anyway, and keeping watch gave her a vague feeling of power over her own destiny.

She heard Reyna murmur something and turned her head to look back at her, staring through the reconfigured geometry of the SUV. It looked like Reyna was already dozing, her eyes heavy. Jeremy was pressed next to her, and her head was nearly resting on his shoulder.

Jeremy was still awake, and he looked back at Courtney from behind her seat. "Hey," he mouthed at her. She smiled back and waved her fingers at him. He reached out and grabbed her hand around the seat. She grabbed his hand back and held it for a moment. Then she remembered she was supposed to be guarding them, so she let go and turned back toward the windshield. The snow had picked up again. She realized at a certain point that the SUV might get buried, although it would have to snow many more feet for that to happen.

Courtney turned back to Jeremy, but now his eyes were shut. She didn't know if he was feigning sleep or what. She wondered why he'd grabbed her hand, but guessed it was stupid to read anything into the gesture. She knew he liked Reyna, not her. It had probably just been a gesture of solidarity or friendship. That was what she was to Jeremy: just a friend.

She brooded as she stared out into the forest and massaged her aching neck. It seemed childish, but thinking about Jeremy kept her mind away from darker images, like the body in the prison van, or the idea that there were crazy people out there in the snow with them.

Her mind wandered, trying to think of what she would do if she were one of the prisoners. Where would she go? Probably hide in the woods somewhere. The prisoners were probably tough. Willing to risk everything to get away. She imagined, in a kind of reverie, that the snow and the cold would be minor obstacles for them. Surely by now they were far away from her and her friends. Perhaps they'd reached a town already.

Just then, Courtney thought she caught a glimpse of movement in the snow, between two impressive pines near the front of the SUV. Her breath stopped, as she stared outward. She told herself it was probably a deer. But the movement hadn't seemed like an animal—it had seemed deliberate and human.

She knew she should whisper back to Jeremy and Reyna that she'd seen something, but she felt petrified, like in a nightmare when her arms and legs grew too heavy to move. As she kept watching, from the edge of one of the trees, she saw a flicker of darkness against the backdrop of snow. A body, thin and ghostlike, but undeniably human, finally emerged.

It was a man, dressed in a gray prison jumpsuit, crawling slowly on his hands and knees. He was headed directly toward Courtney and the SUV.

VI

Courtney silently willed the man to change his course, but he didn't. He continued making unwavering progress, even though his hands and feet were bare, and he was sinking into the snow as he crawled. She couldn't see his face, because his head was hanging down.

Courtney knew that she needed to alert the others, but an odd, hypnotic fascination had taken hold. As she gazed out at the figure, she noticed that he was holding his arms close together, which was limiting his movement in a weird way. It took her a moment to understand that he was wearing handcuffs.

He had snow all over him, and he was shivering in the cold. What little she could see of his skin was as pale and white as the snow itself. His jumpsuit was torn and tattered in places, and dirty with mud and dried blood in others.

Courtney was about to cry out for help, when the man abruptly collapsed in the snow, his arms giving way. His face fell into a snowdrift, and his legs writhed as he tried to push himself back up. It was obvious that he had been outside for a long time. Courtney was relieved he wasn't moving forward anymore. She'd been afraid he was going to crawl right up to the door of the SUV and start banging on it.

Courtney took a jagged breath, trying to calm down, and prepared herself to wake the others. It was then that the man looked up, staring right at Courtney through the windshield.

She couldn't tell if he really saw her or not, but he seemed to be looking right into her eyes, as though he were trying to communicate some sort of urgent message. His face was narrow and angular, kind of gaunt, and there was stubble on his cheeks and chin, along with caked mud. She was surprised by how young he looked, maybe in his early twenties.

His head sank back down in the snow, but his eyes were still staring at her. For a moment she thought he had died, right then and there, with her watching. Then he blinked and she knew he was still alive.

She risked a glance behind her. No one else seemed to be awake. She didn't know why she wasn't yelling and screaming for help yet. Perhaps it was because she felt protected in the cocoon of the SUV, as if the windshield were a barrier between two separate realities. There was no doubt in her mind that the prisoner was one of the men who'd escaped from the van. Possibly he had even killed the guard, yet that seemed unlikely given he was handcuffed and looked close to freezing to death.

The man was no longer moving or doing anything at all. His eyes had drifted away from Courtney and were vaguely focused on some point beyond the SUV. She turned to the back again. In the dark, Reyna's head was still on Jeremy's shoulder, and from their relaxed posture, she could tell they were both sound asleep.

"Rey," she whispered. "Wake up."

Her friend didn't stir.

Courtney looked back at the man, who was still immobile, and then back at Reyna again. "Reyna, wake up," she said, louder. "Someone's outside."

She saw Reyna's eyes struggle open as the girl raised her head wearily, disentangling herself from Jeremy.

"Huh?" Reyna murmured. She impulsively tried to rub one of her eyes, but stopped because she was still wearing gloves.

"Someone's outside," Courtney repeated, softly but firmly. She didn't want to wake the others and have everyone panic. She knew Reyna would be able to handle whatever bad news came their way. "There's a man in the snow, just a few yards from the car." Then she added, "A prisoner."

Reyna looked startled. Without disturbing Jeremy,

she grabbed the side of Courtney's seat and hauled her body forward a little to get a better view. "He looks dead," she whispered when she saw him.

"I don't think so," Courtney replied softly. "He keeps moving."

"How long has he been here? Did you fall asleep?"

Courtney couldn't explain why she hadn't woken Reyna right away, so she shook her head. "He just crawled out of the woods a minute or two ago. Then he fell down and stopped."

"That's crazy."

"I know."

"We have to wake everyone. Jeremy first, then Harris and Melanie." She paused, pushing back a wayward curl of hair from her face. "Do you think he knows we're in here?"

"I'm not sure." Courtney pictured the way he'd stared right at her, but with all the snow, and the reflections from the moonlight on the windshield, she still hoped he hadn't seen her.

"He looks really messed up."

Courtney wondered what would happen if they just ignored the man. She guessed he would die. Would it be murder? Or maybe he was a murderer himself, and it would be justice. Courtney wished she didn't feel so cold, or that her head didn't ache as much, so she could think straight.

"I'll get Jeremy." Reyna slipped back behind Courtney, and Courtney heard her whisper soft words to him.

Courtney was watching the prisoner again. His short-cropped hair was now completely covered with white, so he looked like an old man. She realized if it kept snowing, eventually he would get covered all the way. She shivered, thinking about how it would feel to be smothered by the snow like that.

We can't just let him die out there, she told herself. *No one deserves that. Or do they?*

Jeremy leaned up front to look for himself. He glanced over at Courtney and said, "Reyna told me." His voice sounded thin and tight. "I can't believe this."

"We need to make a decision about what to do, because he's going to die if we don't intervene," Courtney said.

Reyna's whisper came from behind her: "Maybe that's for the best. Who knows? Let me think for a second."

Jeremy added, "We're safe in here for now."

Courtney suddenly realized something. "What if there are other prisoners, and they come looking for him, and then they find us and the SUV? Maybe we'd actually be safer if we brought him inside and hid him."

Jeremy frowned. "I hadn't thought of that."

All three of them heard stirrings from the back, and Harris said grumpily, "What the hell's going on up there?"

"Shhh," Reyna whispered back. "We found one of the prisoners. I mean, he found us."

"For real?" Harris suddenly sounded wide awake. He started trying to scrabble his way forward for a look. Melanie remained slumped behind him.

"Dude, can you keep your voice down?" Jeremy hissed. "He doesn't know we're in here, maybe."

Harris positioned himself precariously in the center of the vehicle and peered through a gap out the windshield. Courtney heard his sharp intake of breath when he saw the man.

Reyna looked back and forth at everyone. "Courtney thinks we should go rescue him. Maybe we should. He might attract the others."

"What? Let's just leave him out there," Harris insisted. "Why the fuck would we go help him?" His head disappeared for a second and then he came back. "Melanie's still sleeping," he said randomly, as though only she could answer the question for him.

"We could get information from the prisoner," Reyna said. "We could find out who else was in the van, and who killed the guard."

"What if he's the killer?" Harris asked.

"Doubtful," Reyna replied. "He's got handcuffs on. And the guard was naked. The killer took his clothes for warmth, I guess. But this guy's got nothing on but his prison outfit."

They were all speaking in low, urgent tones. Courtney's eyes went back to the man in the snow. He wasn't moving at all. She wondered if it was possible that he'd pass away while they were debating his fate. She tried to see if his breath was visible in the snow, but his mouth was pointed down and away from her.

Jeremy spoke up, distracting her. "Listen, this might

sound kind of paranoid, but what if it's a trap?" Courtney and Reyna looked over at him. "What if there's a bunch of them, and they sent this guy to lure us out of the SUV— like a decoy? We go out there to help him, and we get swarmed." His words were greeted with grim silence.

"Our SUV is a total wreck," Reyna pointed out finally. "There's no need for a bunch of convicts to play games with us. They could just attack us straight out."

"I still vote we stay inside," Harris said firmly, although no one had proposed a vote. "Remember, Mel's back there and I have to take care of her. She's hurt."

For some reason, this seemed to annoy Reyna. "Then maybe you should stay here if we go and get the prisoner, okay?"

"Who's we?" Harris said back. "No one has to do what you say."

All the discussion about the prisoner was making Courtney increasingly nervous, but she still trusted her gut instinct that they needed to go save him. Jeremy looked nervous too, his eyes moving back and forth, scanning what little they could see of the forest. Courtney knew if Reyna decided to go, then he would probably side with her. Hoping to spur them both into action, she said, "Time's running out."

Reyna rubbed her eyes and then agreed. "Okay. He's cold, he has handcuffs on. He can't hurt us. At least we can talk to him out there. If he seems safe, then we take him inside. If he's a raving lunatic, then we leave his sorry ass to freeze to death."

"I'll bring the hatchet," Jeremy added. "Just in case." Jeremy turned to Harris, who had disappeared into the back again and was unsuccessfully trying to wake Melanie.

"Stay in here, man. I'll go outside with the girls," Courtney heard Jeremy say.

For once, Harris didn't argue. "Fine. I'll keep watch and come out if you need me." He paused. "I'm having a little trouble waking Mel up. . . ."

"Let her sleep," Reyna called out to him, sounding authoritative. "Sleep will help her get better." Courtney didn't know if this was actually the right idea—she'd heard if someone hit their head it was best to keep them awake—but she didn't feel like challenging her friend at that moment. Besides, the prisoner in the snow was a more immediate crisis.

Courtney climbed into the cavern-like back section of the SUV and looked over at Reyna and Jeremy. They were both pulling their scarves up in preparation for the brutal cold, and Jeremy had the hatchet under his arm.

"Ready?" Reyna asked. She grabbed hold of the door handle, and said, "Help me with this thing." Together, she and Courtney managed to push open the damaged door, forcing it against the fallen snow. A gust of cold air and snow immediately rushed into the vehicle.

"Good luck," Harris muttered as Courtney, Reyna, and Jeremy climbed out one by one into the thick snow that had built up all around the vehicle. The SUV was starting to look like some kind of mutant igloo, Courtney thought. Harris quickly pulled the door shut behind them.

The three friends stood there in the snow, looking toward the man lying in front of the vehicle. He hadn't moved or heard them coming in any way. He was still facedown, his flesh exposed to the elements. Even with her many layers of clothes on, and her hat and her scarf, Courtney was chilled to the bone.

None of them wanted to walk over to the body in the snow, Courtney least of all. She wasn't sure which would be more terrifying at this point: if the man was dead, or if he was still alive.

Reyna took a hesitant step forward, raising her leg with effort, and then sinking it back down in the deep snow. Walking here was as difficult as walking in quicksand. The snow now came up to their thighs. Reyna took another step. Jeremy followed, and then, steeling her nerves, Courtney did the same.

Reyna reached the body first and stood near the man's head, looking down at him. Jeremy and Courtney came around on either side as Harris watched them all through the windshield.

"Hey," Reyna called out to the back of the man's head, her words getting muffled by her scarf. "You okay?" The man didn't move.

"Yo," Jeremy said, louder. There was still nothing. Courtney blinked snow from her eyes.

Jeremy raised his foot out of the snow and nudged the man's shoulder with the toe of his boot. Courtney half expected the man to whip around and grab Jeremy's ankle, but nothing happened.

Reyna crouched down by the man's head and reached out a gloved hand. She tried to lift his head up out of the snow. As she turned and looked back at Courtney, she said, "Help me with him, why don't you—"

Right then, the man emitted an agonized moan. Courtney jumped in surprise.

Equally startled, Reyna dropped his head back down in the snow and took a stumbling step away. "Shit," she swore, looking annoyed that the man had frightened her.

Jeremy was still standing there with the hatchet, an odd stricken look on his face. Perhaps he'd thought the man was already dead.

The man turned his head sideways to gaze at them. He mouthed something, opening and closing his mouth like a dying fish. It took Courtney a moment to realize he was saying "Help me."

"So he's alive," Reyna said, looking not at the man but at Courtney and Jeremy.

"I don't want to touch him," Courtney said, apropos of nothing. Rescuing the prisoner had seemed like a good idea at first, but now she was starting to wonder whether Harris had been right all along.

Reyna stepped up to the man again and knelt down, crouching so she was half immersed in the snow. "We can help you," she said to him. "But you need to give us some information, okay?"

The prisoner started slowly moving his shackled arms. Courtney guessed they were feeling pretty numb. He attempted to push himself up from the snow, but his

eyes kept falling shut, like he was fighting sleep. Courtney knew this was one of the signs of hypothermia, and
figured they'd probably gotten to him just in time.

"Did you shoot that prison guard?" Reyna asked him.
"The one driving the van? We found him naked and
dead, just a mile from here."

Despite the fact that the prisoner scared her, Courtney thought there was something oddly cruel about the
interrogation, something slightly inhumane. The man
seemed to understand the question, though, because
he shook his head and whispered, "No." His voice was
soft and scratchy. Then he mumbled, "I'm so cold. I'm so
cold." He kept moving his arms and managed to roll himself over on his side. Courtney and her companions
stepped back to give him room.

It looked like Jeremy wanted to ask a question or two,
but Reyna kept the lead. "You're an inmate at Maitland
County, right? You were being taken there in that van."

The prisoner nodded, shivering and struggling for
breath. "Yes."

Reyna started peppering him with questions. "What
happened? Who killed the driver? How many prisoners
were in there with you?"

Seemingly too tired to speak again, the man held out
his hands, one with all five fingers outstretched. Courtney thought he was reaching for help, until she realized
he was trying to say there had been five other men on
board.

"And the driver?" Reyna pressed.

The man mouthed something in response, but none of them could hear it. Then he curled up in the fetal position as best he could in the snow, trying to block out the world. The handcuffs glinted under the cold light of the moon. His eyes had fallen shut again.

Reyna turned to the others, exasperated. "Let's get him inside the SUV and warm him up."

In the last two minutes, Courtney's emotions had run the gamut from fear to pity. It was up to them to intervene and save this strange man—no one else could. For all she knew, he could be a serial rapist or a child molester, but to leave him out here would mean imposing a death sentence that he might not deserve.

"We're going to have to pick him up, aren't we?" Courtney asked. Both she and Reyna looked over at Jeremy. As the boy, he was physically the strongest of the three.

He sighed. "You sure we want to do this?"

"Very," Reyna said as Courtney nodded. "We'll help you."

Jeremy handed the hatchet to Reyna. "I just hope he doesn't have AIDS or something," he muttered, as he bent down and prepared to lift the frozen man out of the snow.

"Just don't let him fuck you in the ass, and you'll be okay," Reyna said back.

Jeremy didn't bother replying, but he said to the prisoner, "I'm going to get you up. We're going to take you inside our SUV, where it's warm. Okay? Just relax and let us help you."

The man nodded weakly, his eyes still shut.

Jeremy leaned down over the man's thin frame and grasped his shoulders. He sat him up in the snow, and Courtney and Reyna moved over to assist him. Working together, the three of them managed to get the man fully upright, and they helped him through the snow to the waiting vehicle.

Harris had been watching, and he threw open the door. "That guy looks like a fucking popsicle."

"We're bringing him in," Reyna told him. "Give us a hand, okay?"

Somehow the four of them got the man into the SUV, tumbling him inside and into the back, near Melanie. Harris scrambled over him to protect her.

Courtney climbed in after Jeremy, followed closely by Reyna, who shut the door. The prisoner slumped in a tangled mess against what had once been the side of the vehicle. There wasn't much room for him, or for anyone else. He looked around blearily, as though half asleep. His eyes fixed on Courtney for a moment before sliding away into a dazed, unfocused gaze.

I really hope we made the right decision, Courtney thought, the pit of her stomach tight from nerves. She gazed outside at the imprint his fallen body had left in the snow. She knew that soon it would be filled again, erased by the whiteness, as though he'd never been there at all.

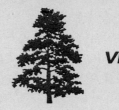

VII

Ten minutes later, the man's eyes were still shut, and he was swimming in and out of consciousness. They had risked turning the dome light on temporarily in order to see him better. He was now swaddled in extra clothes and blankets, wearing a frayed, spare pair of Jeremy's jeans, three layers of socks, and a wool cap. Because of the handcuffs, they hadn't been able to get any shirts over his arms, so they just draped him in sweatshirts, and wrapped a jacket around him, zipping it up with his arms inside.

When they'd been dressing him, Courtney had noticed through the thin, wet jumpsuit that his white skin was covered in black tattoos. Reyna had pointed at one of them adorning his back, and said, "Aryan brotherhood." No one else had commented, although the tattoos scared Courtney. She had to remind herself that even though this man was handcuffed and helpless right now, he was probably violent and dangerous. The tattoos were not a good sign.

Now they were all waiting for the prisoner to start speaking and tell them what had happened in that van. Reyna tried to give him some sips of Gatorade to wake him up, but the liquid just dribbled down his chin.

Courtney examined the prisoner's face. He looked even younger close up, but rough around the edges. There were lines and creases on his face that probably shouldn't have been there, she thought. But he looked relaxed now in his exhaustion, and there was a softness to the cast of his face. His lips were pursed in a pout, vaguely feminine. Even in the dim light, Courtney could see that his eyes, whenever they flickered open, were pale gray-blue.

"This is crazy," Harris said to Jeremy. He had a protective arm around the slumbering Melanie. "You shouldn't have brought this guy in here."

"We didn't have a choice in the end," Reyna said. Courtney noticed she was watching the prisoner's face too.

Harris sighed angrily. "We're giving him warmth, and a place to rest. He probably doesn't deserve it. If he wakes up and tries anything, I'm going to kick his—"

"Stop," Courtney interrupted. She'd noticed that the prisoner's eyes were now fully open, and staying that way. "I think he's awake again."

Harris squinted at him. "Is that so."

The prisoner struggled to say something and made a coughing, gagging sound. Reyna brought up the Gatorade bottle and he managed to take a tentative sip, like an infant. Then he lay back against the hull, watching the four of them cluster around him.

"Where . . . Where am I?" he finally managed to ask softly, in a hoarse voice. Courtney thought he sounded vulnerable and scared.

"You're in our SUV," Reyna said. "We rescued you."

The prisoner licked his cracked lips, as his eyes moved slowly around his surroundings and lit upon Reyna's face.

"We hit a deer and crashed," Jeremy explained awkwardly. "There was a blizzard. We're stuck here until morning . . ." His words trailed off because he saw that the prisoner wasn't listening. The man was still watching Reyna.

"I shouldn't be here," he said slowly.

"What do you mean by that?" Reyna asked.

The man didn't answer, but he was still staring at her. Courtney thought it was vaguely creepy.

"You crawled out of the snow," Reyna continued. "Remember? We took you inside so you wouldn't die out there."

Harris shifted uneasily against the side of the van. Courtney could tell the prisoner was unnerving him the most.

"We could have let you die," Harris said. When the

man didn't look at him, Harris said, louder, "Hey, ass-hole, we could have let you die. You owe us."

The prisoner finally looked at him. He swallowed hard, his Adam's apple bobbing up and down, and said, "Thank you." Then he shut his eyes. "I don't remember how I got here. The prison van stopped because of the snow. I remember there was a fight—" He suddenly stopped talking, and his face scrunched up. "My feet," he gasped. "They're killing me! They hurt so bad." Courtney knew he was in pain only because his freezing limbs were starting to warm up. She remained fascinated and terrified by his presence.

"Listen to me," Reyna said, leaning in close to him as he tried to massage his feet. "This is really important. I asked already, but I want to make sure. How many people were in that van with you?"

"Six, including the guard who was driving," he said, moving his legs around. "There were five of us in back."

"And you didn't kill the driver?" Reyna asked bluntly.

The prisoner looked a little startled by the question. "No." He poked his hands out from under the borrowed jacket, displaying his handcuffs. "See?"

"That doesn't mean you didn't do it," Harris blurted. "Right? You can still kill someone even if you've got handcuffs on."

The prisoner's eyes were roaming again and this time they found Courtney. She wanted to look away, but for some reason she was able to hold his gaze. Reyna was telling Harris to shut up, but a question occurred to Courtney, so she cut through the noise.

"What's your name?" she asked him. There was a brief moment of silence. No one else had thought, or cared, to ask that question.

"Everyone calls me J.G.," he finally said. He smiled crookedly. Courtney knew he hadn't really answered the question. "What's your handle?"

Courtney told him her first name, but not her last, and the others grudgingly followed suit.

"So what happened in the van, J.G.?" Reyna asked. "If you didn't kill the driver, who did?"

"Yeah," Jeremy echoed wanly. "Tell us."

J.G. looked past them through the windshield, out into the snow. "You don't want to know."

"Sure we do," Harris said. "Because if you don't start talking, I'm going to think you did it, and then I'm going to toss you back out in the snow to die, understand?"

"I understand." His voice was getting stronger. J.G. tried to move himself into a more comfortable position, his thin body arching forward. "These cuffs," he said. "You don't have a way to take them off me, do you?"

"Don't even think about that now," Reyna said. "Tell us what happened and then we'll see."

The prisoner looked hesitant. "You won't like what you hear."

"Try me."

"Well, when the van broke down, a couple guys in back started a fight," he said. "The guard panicked and threatened to start shooting. But four of us didn't pose any real problem for him. Only one guy did. Leonard Bell." He paused. "Ever heard of him?"

"No," Reyna said. The name was unfamiliar to Courtney too. She glanced around at the others, who all looked blank-faced.

"Shit, don't you guys watch TV?" J.G. asked. "A couple years back, Leonard Bell killed almost his entire family. His mom, his dad, and his two younger brothers. Cut them right up, and then he ate part of his sister. But he let her live and she went insane. He's a stone-cold psychopathic serial killer. He was being taken to Maitland Correctional with me and the other unlucky suckers in that van."

"Are you fucking kidding me?" Harris asked slowly.

J.G. shook his head.

In the horrified silence that followed, Courtney knew her companions were all wondering what awful things J.G. might have done to end up alongside someone like Leonard. She certainly was.

J.G. must have sensed it too, because he laughed. The sound was dry and without mirth, more like a cough than anything else. "Don't worry. I was in for drug possession and dealing. Crystal meth. Three strikes and you're out. It was the same with one of the other guys. The other two had beaten up their wives or some domestic crap like that. Leonard was the only one who'd killed anyone."

"So this Leonard character—assuming he exists—he

murdered the guard?" Reyna asked, in full trial mode. Courtney glanced over at Jeremy, who was watching but not saying much.

The prisoner nodded in response to Reyna's question. "The guard made a mistake. He used the CB for help, but it was out because of the storm. During the fight, Leonard got one of the other guys around the neck and said he was going to kill him. The guard opened up the back to restrain Leonard, and he let that maniac get too close. Leonard grabbed the guard's rifle and pumped a round of lead into his belly. Then he shot him a few more times in the chest, just to make sure. He got the keys off the body, unlocked his handcuffs, and put on the guard's clothes. He kept waving the gun around, so I took off running. I was out of there lickety-split." He paused. "I don't know what happened to the others. . . ."

"Why were you on this road anyway?" Reyna asked. "It's not exactly a major highway."

"Local shortcut, I guess. Probably so the guard could take a longer cigarette break. We were being transferred from downstate to Maitland, 'cause of overcrowding."

J.G.'s story sounded so crazy, Courtney didn't know if he was telling the truth or not. But either way she was terrified. It was very possible that a complete madman was out there in the snow, armed with a rifle. And if J.G. had managed to find them, then presumably so could Leonard. Yet it was also possible J.G. was a total liar.

"You're telling us the truth about everything?" Courtney pressed.

"Why would I lie?"

"I can think of a few reasons," Reyna added.

J.G. calmly returned Reyna's fierce gaze. "I've got nothing to hide. In fact, I've got nothing at all. Look at me. No clothes, no rifle, no food. Nothing. I'm grateful that you took me in."

Harris turned aggressive again. "What if there's no Leonard and you killed that guard, huh? Are we supposed to take the word of some racist, drug-dealing hick?"

Jeremy tried to calm him down. "It doesn't matter right now if we believe him or not. As long as no one else gets hurt."

"Someone's going to get hurt if he keeps saying stupid shit like that," Harris snapped back.

"Please," Courtney said, trying to hold off a pointless argument between Jeremy and Harris. "Fight about it later."

"I'm telling the truth," J.G. insisted softly. "Leonard is out there, and I'm in here. I won't cause any problems for you." Courtney wasn't sure what he meant by that, but he elaborated: "I've never done a violent thing in my life. I'm a convict because of my addiction to meth. I learned what all addicts learn in the end, that no one is stronger than their addictions. I won't hurt anyone."

"That's right you won't," Harris said.

J.G. smiled grimly again, like Harris was amusing him. "Don't waste time worrying about me, son. Don't make the same mistake our guard did. Leonard is about six foot four and two hundred pounds of muscle and mental insanity. And I'm sure he's looking to put his rifle to good use."

The atmosphere in the SUV had become increasingly tense. Courtney wasn't sure whether she believed J.G. or not, but she knew that in his condition, with the five of them around him, it would be difficult for him to try anything suspicious even if he wanted to.

Courtney's back was hurting, so she slumped against the opposite side of the driver's seat. It was then that Melanie unexpectedly lurched forward on the other side of the group and fell against Harris. Everyone twitched in surprise, even J.G.

"Jesus, Mel," Harris said, trying to help. "You okay?"

Melanie looked very far from okay. Her face had gone white and her eyes were partly rolled up in her head, the pupils almost disappearing into her skull.

"She's having a seizure," Reyna said, moving forward across the dark space. In the SUV they were all so tightly entwined it felt like a nightmare game of Twister.

Harris grabbed his girlfriend and said, "Mel!" When he pulled his hand back, Courtney could see it was wet with blood. "She's bleeding!" he said, the shock evident in his voice. Courtney felt stunned. Melanie continued to spasm as Harris held her.

"Bleeding from where?" Reyna asked, her voice controlled. Her hands moved up and down Melanie's body.

"I don't know!" Harris said. "God, there's blood everywhere."

"Why didn't she say anything?" Jeremy asked.

Courtney tried to get a good look at Melanie. Harris was pushing up her shirt to look for any sort of wound, while Reyna was checking her head. Courtney was wondering over and over how they could have missed something this serious.

We were so preoccupied with J.G., she thought. *We forgot about Melanie.*

Courtney's eyes flicked over to J.G., and she saw that he was silently taking in the terrifying scene. His face was impassive, and his eyes displayed no emotion. Their color, which had first seemed exotic, now reminded her of concrete.

Courtney tried to slide around to get closer to Melanie. Harris wasn't finding any sign of a wound on her back or chest, even though he was using his cigarette lighter to help him see because the dome light was so dim. There were some bruises forming from the impact, but Melanie's skin was unbroken. Courtney saw that the floor of the SUV was dark with blood, difficult to see at first in the light, but now unmistakable. The blood had been pooling up behind Melanie while she rested.

Melanie's head was tilted back against the side of the SUV. She was pale and struggling to breathe as she came around. "What's happening to me?" she asked in a plaintive wail.

"You're going to be okay," Reyna told her.

"I can't find anything," Harris said, sounding near tears. "But there's so much blood."

Reyna was at his side, helping get Melanie's clothes off. "Stay calm. We'll find it. We can stop the bleeding."

Courtney wanted to help too, in some tangible way, but she didn't know what to do. She felt paralyzed by fear, and by her own ignorance. She felt guilty she didn't have the ability to step in and fix everything, and take control of a crisis. She was always afraid she'd just make things worse.

She noticed that Jeremy was just watching too, with a look of stupefaction on his face. He's probably thinking the same things I am, she thought.

Harris and Reyna had Melanie's jacket and shirts off and were now working on her jeans as she sprawled across the cargo hold.

"It's cold," Melanie was saying, clutching helplessly at her partially exposed chest.

Courtney had a frightening thought, one too awful to dwell on for more than a second: What if Melanie's bleeding was internal, and the blood was coming out of her from the inside, between her legs.

Then Reyna finally said, "I see it! There's something on her thigh. Look."

They all craned forward to see, Harris leaning in with the lighter. The inside of Melanie's jeans was soaked with blood. On the side of her left thigh was a round puncture wound, nearly the size of a quarter. Blood was leaking out of it slowly, had probably been leaking out for some time.

Melanie made a strange gasping noise, like she was

about to throw up or pass out. Reyna grabbed her head and held it, while Courtney, Harris, and Jeremy inspected the wound.

"It—it could be an artery," Jeremy stammered, looking almost as pale as Melanie. "I remember from bio class."

"Or a nicked vein," Reyna mused. "It's not coming out too fast."

"It looks serious," Harris said urgently.

"It is."

Courtney spoke up: "Don't we need to put a tourniquet on it?" She looked at Reyna for confirmation. "To stop the bleeding?"

Reyna nodded and said, "I think so." She was still analyzing. "Sometimes that's not the right thing to do. It might compress the blood vessels and hurt her leg for good if we leave it on too long."

"But it's an emergency," Harris said. "She can't just keep bleeding like this. She can't have that much blood left!"

"I feel sick," Melanie whispered to him.

Harris ran a hand through her thick hair. "You're going to be okay, sweetie. I love you, okay? I love you." He had her blood all over his fingers.

Reyna started rummaging for a spare T-shirt, presumably to wrap around the girl's leg. Courtney realized none of them knew the first thing about how to treat a wound like Melanie's, not even Reyna. If Melanie died, that would change everything. There would be no going back from that.

In the tense silence, the prisoner suddenly spoke.

"I can help her," he said, his voice very calm. Those were the first words he'd said since Melanie's seizure.

Courtney and the others turned to look at him. He had propped himself up in the corner and was staring at them. The wind made an ominous droning noise outside, and Courtney knew the storm was picking up.

"I can help your friend," J.G. said again. He shook his shackled wrists, deliberately making the cuffs jangle. "But first you have to help me."

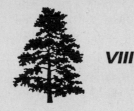

VIII

When the surprise had worn off, Harris snarled, "How the hell are you going to help her? You distracted us. If it weren't for you, we would have found out she was hurt sooner. You shouldn't even be here."

J.G. wasn't disturbed by the hostility. "I can help because I trained as a medic in the army," he said, his voice flat.

"The army?" Harris snapped. "Then why were you in prison? Shouldn't you be off killing Arabs somewhere?"

Reyna turned to the prisoner. "Tell us what to do."

J.G. jangled the handcuffs again. "First, you need to get these off me. I can't be useful with my hands tied up."

"No way," Reyna said, beating Harris to it. "That's the last thing we're going to do. There's no reason we should trust you yet. Tell us how to help Melanie, and then we'll talk."

J.G. shook his head. "The cuffs need to come off first."

Courtney felt a sudden surge of anger at the man who they'd been kind enough to rescue. Surprising herself with the strength in her voice, she stared him down and said, "How do you think we could even get those things off you? We don't have a key, okay?"

J.G. swung his head to look at her. His face was red and abraded in places, thawing from the deep freeze of the snow. "You don't need a key," he said. "It's a myth that handcuffs aren't breakable, especially state-issued ones. You could get these off with a steak knife. You could pick the lock. Or if you got some kind of tire iron, or fire axe . . ."

"Why would we have a fire axe, douche bag?" Harris asked. "This isn't a fire truck."

Courtney immediately thought of the hatchet, but she said nothing.

"Harris," Jeremy said. "Quit stressing. We're not taking his handcuffs off."

"That's right," Reyna told the prisoner firmly. "Look at it from our perspective. If our positions were reversed, would you trust any of us?"

J.G. was silent.

"Thought so," Reyna retorted.

Melanie moaned softly in the back, shifting against the clothing now sticky with her drying blood. Courtney could hear the sound of Melanie's skin pulling against the fabric, like someone tugging on a strip of Velcro. Melanie was struggling to get her jacket back on, semi-comatose. Her jeans were still off, the wound exposed near the V of her crotch.

"Help her," Harris commanded the prisoner, although he couldn't keep a note of pleading desperation from his voice. "If you really were a medic, then you can fix her."

J.G. sighed. Courtney felt as though she could sense the thoughts shifting and swirling behind his eyes. "Okay," he finally said. "Fine. You need to do exactly what I tell you." He looked away from Harris, and his eyes found Courtney. "I want her to do it," he said.

"Me?" Courtney asked, surprised he hadn't picked Reyna.

"Yes. You're going to be my hands. Only you—no one else."

This edict made Courtney uneasy. The last thing she wanted to do was follow the instructions of a convict. And on another level, she was afraid of the responsibility. "Reyna wants to be a doctor. She should do it."

J.G. shook his head. "I want you."

No one said anything, or asked J.G. why he'd chosen Courtney. Harris, Jeremy, and Reyna just sat back and stared at her. Thanks guys, Courtney thought.

J.G. struggled to get all the way upright, so that he was leaning over, staring down at Melanie's injured leg. "There's probably a tear in her femoral artery. That puncture wound looks deep enough to have reached it, and she's hemorrhaging." He looked back at Courtney. "I need you to palpate the wound for me, to feel and see if anything's in there."

He said the words so clinically, it took Courtney a second to realize that he wanted her to feel inside the hole in Melanie's leg.

"You've got to be kidding me," she muttered.

"Won't that just make things worse?" Reyna interrupted. "Won't that just put an infection in there?"

Jeremy and Harris were both silent.

J.G. was undaunted. "If there's shrapnel from the accident inside, we need to get it out. If we leave it, things will be far worse." He turned back to Courtney. "After you check the wound, you'll need to pack it. Snow is the best thing we've got. Maybe one of you others can open the door and grab a handful. The snow will fill the wound and shrink the blood vessels, which will stop the bleeding. Then we'll apply a tourniquet. Not too tight, just enough to help stop the blood flow. After that, we lay her down, and elevate the leg. She should stabilize."

Courtney was glad J.G. sounded so extremely rational and articulate. She only hoped he knew what he was talking about.

"Of course if you got these cuffs off, I could do all this myself, faster and better. I have experience."

His words went unanswered.

Reyna looked over at Courtney. "You can do this, Court," she said, like a deranged cheerleader.

"Do I have a choice?" It was strange that J.G. had insisted on her, Courtney thought, almost like he was trying to establish a bond between the two of them. *Good luck, buddy.*

Courtney took in a deep breath and exhaled slowly, trying to calm herself. She moved past the others, clambering over the detritus of the accident to Melanie, as Harris scooted aside to make room.

Courtney looked over at J.G. From her new vantage point she could see there were dark circles ringing both his eyes. He looked tired but focused. "What now?" she asked.

He held the index and middle fingers of his right hand together. "Go like this, then press your fingers around the wound firmly. See if you feel anything hard, anything unusual."

Courtney didn't know if she'd be able to tell what "unusual" was. As her companions watched in horrified fascination, she stripped off her gloves, took her bare fingers, and pressed at the edges of the circular hole in Melanie's leg. She was afraid the slow leak of blood would accelerate with pressure, but it didn't. Melanie moved her leg slightly, but her eyes remained shut, and her head fell backward against the SUV's ruined hull.

"Good," J.G. said, watching closely. "Feel anything strange?"

Courtney shook her head. The flesh of Melanie's thigh felt firm, but normal. The ends of Courtney's fingers were slick with blood.

"Now take your index finger and place it in the wound.

You're looking for a foreign object. We need to know if whatever caused that injury is still inside her."

Bile rose in Courtney's throat, but she forced it back down, trying to quell her visceral reaction of disgust. She told herself to get over her squeamishness and concentrate on helping Melanie. The tip of her finger slowly entered the wound, tentatively sliding into the opening. Melanie moved her position slightly, making weak noises of pain, and Courtney paused, feeling sick. She looked away from her hand and at the side of the SUV, trying to find some happier thoughts to fixate on. There were none.

"Is the wound clear?" J.G. asked.

Without looking down, Courtney probed deeper. It was spongy and warm inside. She tried to tell herself she wasn't feeling the insides of a human body, but it didn't work. Suddenly overcome by nausea, she yanked her finger out and wiped her hand violently on the seat.

"It's clear," she managed to say. She looked back at the others, trying not to gag. Reyna was watching intensely, taking in the whole scene. Harris was watching too, but he looked as ill as Courtney felt. His lips were moving, and he was saying words under his breath. Courtney realized that he was praying. Jeremy was turned around, looking out the windshield. It had obviously been too much for him.

"Nice work," J.G. said, his voice as cold as the temperature outside. "Now you need to pack that wound. Someone get her some snow."

"I'll do it," Jeremy said, perhaps trying to make up for his failure of nerve.

He dislodged a suitcase blocking a broken side window, and passed Courtney a gloved handful, almost reverentially. She took some in her blood-drenched fingers, and gritting her teeth, pressed it into Melanie's wound.

Melanie writhed, arching her back in pain and making a hissing sound.

"You're doing good," J.G. murmured to Courtney. "You might have just saved your friend's life." He closed his eyes. "Remember to tie something around her leg, an inch or more above the wound. And get it elevated. She'll have to get that laceration sutured at some point."

The others moved in to help as Courtney slumped back, away from Melanie's prone body. "I need to wash my hands," she said.

"I'll get you some more snow," Jeremy told her quietly. He moved the suitcase again and got her some. She scrubbed her hands with it, feeling them get even more numb than they already were, if such a thing was possible. She dried them on her jeans and then got her gloves back on quickly. She felt exhausted from the physical and emotional turmoil of the last few hours.

Harris and Reyna were repositioning Melanie. Her upper torso was now lying flat, and her legs were elevated on a duffel bag. She was very pale, but the bleeding looked like it had stopped.

Harris turned to J.G. "Will she be okay?"

The prisoner's thin body was hunched up in the corner again. "It depends how much blood she lost. Keep giving her Gatorade."

Harris nodded. "Okay." He turned back to tend to her some more.

J.G. paused for a moment and then raised his shackled hands under his jacket. "I don't suppose . . ."

Reyna turned around and said, "No. We're grateful you helped Melanie, but that doesn't change anything."

J.G. looked vaguely aggravated, but he lowered his hands.

"Mel's breathing is really shallow," Harris said suddenly. "Worse than before. We need to get her to a hospital."

"I don't think that's going to happen anytime soon," J.G. volunteered, curling his legs up under him. "There aren't any hospitals around here, believe me. Not for a long ways."

"How do you know?" Courtney challenged, annoyed by the way he sounded almost smug.

"Because I grew up nearby, in Waterville. I went to high school probably just thirty miles from this spot, give or take a few."

"Are you serious?" Reyna asked, surprised.

J.G. nodded. It was slowly dawning on Courtney and the others that if what J.G. had said was true, then he might be able to guide them out of this mess.

Reyna leaned forward, peering at J.G. with dark eyes. "Then you know how to get out of here? Why didn't you say so?"

He grimaced. "No one asked me. I thought you'd have maps."

"We don't." Reyna sounded defensive.

"Do you know where the closest town is?" Courtney asked him.

"I should. It's called Pine Valley, and it's near the pen, where that prison van was taking me. It's about thirteen miles away."

"That's not too far," Reyna said. Courtney could see the calculations going on behind her eyes.

"Thirteen miles is far in a blizzard," Jeremy pointed out.

"Ten miles of it are right on the road," J.G. elaborated. "But for the last three, we'd have to cut across the side of a mountain and walk through the woods to get there. See, the prison is on this road, but the town itself isn't. It's farther west."

"But If the journey's mostly on the road, that means we could do it," Reyna said, sounding excited. "We could leave Harris here with Mel, and the rest of us could leave now, and we'd—"

"No. We can't go anywhere in the dark," J.G. said urgently, talking over her. Courtney noticed his voice had changed. There was an unmistakable note of fear in it for the first time. "It's too dangerous. Leonard might be out there. If you wait until morning, I'll guide you."

Harris had been listening to their conversation from the back and said, "If we wait too long, Mel might not make it." He sounded choked up. Courtney knew it must be a brutal experience to watch his girlfriend suffer like this. Courtney shared in the feeling, and only wished she could do something more to help.

J.G. eyed Courtney and the others solemnly. "If we leave this car, and we run into Leonard Bell, then we definitely won't make it. We'll end up like that bastard driving the prison van. Maybe worse for you girls."

Courtney and Reyna looked at each other.

"Why'd he let you go, anyway?" Reyna asked J.G. finally. "If Leonard's so crazy, I mean."

"I don't know. I was ready to fight if he pointed the rifle my way, but he didn't. He was saving bullets, probably. He thought I'd die in the snow."

They digested his words in the ensuing silence. Outside, Courtney saw that the snow was falling heavily again.

"Morning's not far away," Reyna said, rubbing the back of her neck. She glanced at her watch. "Just a couple hours. Everything will be different in the daylight. Even if it's still snowing, we'll be able to see better." She paused. "If Leonard's out there, we'll have more of a chance." She looked at J.G. and added, "Assuming Leonard really does exist."

J.G. stared back at her, unblinking, and said, "I wish he didn't."

"So we stick to our original plan and wait for the sun," Reyna declared. "And then some of us will go for help again."

Courtney and Jeremy nodded.

J.G. rubbed the side of his face thoughtfully, massaging the raw skin. "You're making the right choice," he said flatly.

Somehow his words didn't set Courtney's mind at ease. In fact, they did the opposite. She prayed that Melanie would survive the final dark hours of the night, and that they hadn't made the wrong decision.

IX

The sky began to lighten almost two and a half hours later. At first it was a nearly imperceptible shading of the clouds and the snow, but soon it became apparent that the sun was indeed struggling to rise. The snow continued to fall, casting a pall over the landscape. Neither Courtney nor any of the others had slept since J.G.'s arrival.

Courtney tried to find the courage within herself for what she knew would be a difficult journey. *Thirteen miles in a blizzard.* She thought about how hard it had been when she and Reyna had pressed just one mile ahead and discovered the van. Thirteen miles through the snow-swept wilderness would take a lot of effort, and she already felt spent from the traumas of the night before. She was very cold, and tried not to think about how freezing it would be outside the womblike confines of the SUV.

Courtney knew that Melanie was not doing well. She had survived the night but seemed to be drifting on the edge of unconsciousness again. Harris and Jeremy looked exhausted too. Courtney noticed that only Reyna and J.G. looked somewhat alert, and ready to face the challenges of the day.

"You sure you know where the town is?" Reyna asked J.G. as she bundled up in preparation for the journey. She and Courtney had packed two backpacks with Gatorade, snack food, and some matches they had unearthed. They had also decided to bring the hatchet with them for protection.

J.G. nodded tersely at Reyna's words. "I'm not aiming to get us lost out there."

Jeremy looked like he wanted to say something. "Hey, J.G.—" he managed, and then stopped, like he was uncomfortable.

J.G. looked over at him. "Yeah?"

"You're not going to, like, run off on us or anything, are you?"

"Why would I do that?"

Jeremy hesitated. "I don't know. Maybe it's weird you're so eager to help us get to Pine Valley. Won't they lock you back up?"

"Sure, but at least I won't get a murder rap pinned on me. If I don't turn myself in, they'll think I helped Leonard kill that guard. Running is what guilty people do. I've got a fifteen-year sentence right now, but I could be out in eight with good behavior. It'd be life with no parole if they stuck me with murder."

Courtney peered over at him. "Why would they charge you with a crime if you're innocent?"

J.G. forced a laugh. "You don't know much about our legal system, do you? You've still got faith in things." He shook his head. "If they can't find Leonard, it'll be me that takes the fall. Someone always has to. That's how things work in this country. No one gives a rat's ass about a guy like me."

"Well, just don't try to run, or misdirect us, or strand us out there, okay?" Reyna said.

"With these cuffs on, I wouldn't get very far, would I?" Then he added defiantly: "I'm disappointed you don't trust me."

"We'll trust you when we get there," Reyna said. "You have to earn our trust. No games." Reyna looked over at Courtney. "Court, you ready?"

"Not really," she replied, "but I guess it doesn't matter." She knew she would never be ready. She curled her throbbing toes in her boots.

"Let's get this show on the road." Reyna shouldered open the passenger door, letting a gust of freezing air and snow penetrate the vehicle. She climbed out clutching a backpack, followed by Jeremy and the hatchet, and then Courtney with the second pack. All three of them murmured their good-byes to Harris, who accepted them as somberly as condolences. J.G.

climbed out the door last, but struggled to find his footing because he couldn't use his arms for balance. Jeremy grabbed him and helped pull him out into the snow. Then Jeremy shut the door to the SUV, sealing Harris and Melanie inside.

Outside the vehicle, it was colder than Courtney had imagined possible, and she felt a pang of longing for the warmth and comfort of home, a place that now seemed like a cruel mirage. She wondered what her parents were doing—no doubt they'd already called the police by now and were searching for her. Except they were probably searching the wrong road. No one would have expected them to take this winding, rural route.

Courtney tried not to think about home too much, because she was afraid she might break down and start crying. She forced herself to keep her parents and all the things she loved out of her mind. Instead, she stood there shivering, moving her feet up and down in a desperate effort to stay warm. She saw Reyna doing the same thing. Even J.G. was shivering, despite the layers of clothes wrapped around him. Scabs had formed over the abrasions on his face.

"Son of a bitch," J.G. cursed as he pounded his borrowed boots into the snow, his breath visible with every exhalation. "It's colder than a pimp's heart out here." Courtney didn't know if he was trying to be funny, or if it was some sort of prison expression. He didn't look as frail as he had the night before—if anything, he seemed oddly invigorated by the cold—but he looked very thin, and impossibly white, like a cadaver.

Courtney saw that Jeremy was massaging his ribs like they were hurting him again. She wondered if the four of them could actually make it thirteen miles, but then she reminded herself there weren't any other options. The road was probably closed, and Melanie was badly hurt, and no one was coming to save them. They would have to save themselves.

Reyna's face was mostly hidden by her wool cap and her scarf, which she'd wrapped around her nose and mouth like a mask. "C'mon, J.G.," she called out, the words getting muffled. "Take us to Pine Valley."

J.G. nodded and began walking back up to the road, so Courtney and her two friends followed. Walking was hard; Courtney's joints were stiff and sore, and the cold weather didn't help them feel any better. She'd dried out in the SUV, but now the damp was seeping back in. Luckily, her backpack wasn't too heavy, so it didn't weigh her down much. They reached the tree-lined road and continued walking, heading north again.

Everything ached from the accident, and from being confined in the uncomfortable SUV. The two lumps on Courtney's head were now the size of half-dollars. She entertained a brief fantasy that maybe she could turn back and stay with Harris and Melanie in the SUV, but she understood it would be worse in some ways to remain stranded and waiting in the car. At least this way she was taking action and doing something to help herself.

As she walked, sandwiched between Reyna and Jeremy, Courtney realized they would have to pass the prison van again, and the corpse inside it. She hoped that none of them would want to stop and look inside. She didn't want to go anywhere near that van or its awful contents.

Courtney's muscles were already begging for rest, but she refused to give in to the pain. It was easy to take each step down into the snow, but bringing each foot up again was agony on her knees and thighs. She wondered if Jeremy and Reyna felt the same way. She could tell that they were both struggling, from the ragged sounds of their breathing and because they were moving at such a slow crawl. Only J.G. seemed to be negotiating the snow with ease, his thin legs moving up and down like pistons. If he felt any discomfort from the handcuffs, he wasn't showing it.

Courtney looked around her, hoping the surroundings would distract from her pain. But there was no break in the thick forests of Douglas fir on either side of the deserted road. She felt disoriented by the uniform whiteness of the trees, the road, and the cloud-filled sky. If it weren't for the snowflakes that fell down on her, she might not have known which way was up.

As Courtney struggled onward, all kinds of strange and unexpected thoughts flooded into her mind. She found herself dwelling on the stupidest, smallest things,

things that didn't even matter anymore. She thought of Reyna's casual dismissal of Jeremy and his journal, like he was no one to her. Reyna had once told Courtney that she'd never really been in love. Courtney didn't know whether to admire her on that count, or feel sorry for her. There were plenty of guys who were into Reyna, but she seemed deliberately oblivious to all of them, as though none of them were good enough for her.

Courtney remembered that at the ski lodge, Jeremy had tried to flirt with Reyna, in his goofy way. They had all been drunk and hanging out around the hot tub, but Reyna hadn't been interested in him at all. There was a coolness and a hardness to her that was sometimes puzzling, even slightly scary.

Courtney's mind drifted to J.G., who was still forging the trail several paces ahead of them. She couldn't even imagine what it was like to be inside his head. He was a felon, a drug dealer, and, judging from his tattoos, a racist—a seemingly unrepentant bad person. Yet here he was, leading them to safety. They needed one another: he would have frozen to death without them, and they would be lost without him. It was an uneasy alliance, and Courtney only hoped that nothing would go awry and tip the balance in the wrong direction.

Half an hour later they reached the abandoned prison van. Courtney's hopes of passing it by were dashed when J.G. headed straight toward it. But then he paused and veered slightly to the left, breaking into a sudden loping run.

Courtney felt her stomach sink. Was he running away from them already?

"What the hell is he doing?" Reyna muttered in annoyance.

The three of them followed quickly after the prisoner, who was now twenty paces ahead. Courtney worried all of a sudden that maybe J.G. had found the missing rifle in the snow. She knew it was unlikely, and wondered if he could even load and fire a rifle with his handcuffs on, but she didn't want to take any chances.

The same thing must have occurred to Reyna, because she picked up speed and started yelling at J.G., "Hey, stop! Stop running!"

He finally slowed down and turned around to look back at the panicked group rushing toward him. "Relax," he called out. "But take a look at this."

Courtney reached him a few seconds after Reyna did, and she stood there panting and gasping for air in the cold. Jeremy was at her side.

J.G. had indeed discovered something, but it wasn't the missing rifle. In some ways it was stranger and more disturbing.

"Now that's just plain weird," Reyna breathed, as they all looked down at the snow.

Someone had carved two deep intersecting lines into it, each several feet long, so that they formed the unmistakable shape of a crucifix. The lines were half a foot in width, like miniature trenches, and so deep that they penetrated all the way to the icy crust that covered the road's surface.

Courtney knelt down and inspected the strange artifact. "It's fresh," she said. "Someone just did this, or it'd be filled with snow already."

"If it's fresh, where are the footprints?" Reyna asked.

"Good question."

Jeremy was looking around in all directions, casting his eyes over the walls of white trees as he held the hatchet tightly.

J.G. paused only for a beat until he said the words Courtney had been dreading: "Leonard Bell did this."

"How do you know?" Reyna challenged. "It could have been someone else who was in that van with you. There were five of you, right? How do you know it was Leonard?"

J.G. gazed back at her coolly. His expression was difficult for Courtney to read. "I just know."

When Courtney spoke, her words felt creaky and slow. "Why would Leonard, or anyone, waste his time digging a cross in the snow?"

"To scare people," J.G. replied. "To mess with their minds." He shielded his eyes with his hands as he stared off down the road. "That's what guys like Leonard do. I've met enough psychos in the pen to know how their heads work. He covered his tracks somehow."

"Why did he make a cross?" Courtney asked, confused. It wasn't a very scary symbol. "Is Leonard religious?"

J.G. shook his head. "In prison, a crucifix symbolizes death. That someone's going to get killed." When he saw they didn't understand, he elaborated: "It comes from death row, when the priest administers last rites. It's not a good sign. It brings only bad things, like a curse . . . if you believe in that kind of stuff."

Reyna broke in. "Well, I have a question. Why would Leonard still be hanging around here when he's murdered someone? Shouldn't he be on the run, or hiding out? It doesn't make sense to me."

"Someone who cuts up and eats part of his sister isn't rational," J.G. said slowly. "Maybe one murder's not enough for Leonard this week. Maybe he wants more." He paused. "For all we know, he's keeping a scorecard."

Courtney didn't like where this conversation was headed. She stared back down at the cross dug into the snow. Her eyes were aching from the glare of perpetual whiteness. "But how does Leonard know anyone would find this thing? Does he know we're out here?" The knot in Courtney's stomach had turned into a full-fledged sick feeling that threatened to overwhelm her.

"We might want to consider turning back," J.G. said after a pause.

"We can't," Reyna told him. "We need to get help for Melanie. Besides, if Leonard knows about us, then he could track us back to the SUV anyway. We have to keep going forward."

Jeremy didn't say anything, so Courtney said, "Rey, I don't know if that's a good idea. At the SUV we have some protection, and safety in numbers. Out here we're just easy targets."

Reyna frowned at her. "Do you want Melanie to die?"

"No, of course not," Courtney retorted. "But I don't want us to die either. Do you? If we die, then no one's going to help Mel anyway."

Jeremy cleared his throat and said nervously, "Uh, Court, I guess I think we should keep going too."

Courtney was fed up with him. "Are you saying that because you really believe it, or because you want to impress Reyna?" She saw his cheeks redden a little, and not from cold, but she didn't care if she was embarrassing him. "This is life or death, Jer. There's a crazy person out here with a gun. Think about it. Don't just agree with Reyna all the time because you have a crush on her. Come on. What do you really want to do?"

Jeremy looked wounded. He glanced away, mumbling something under his breath as he shouldered the hatchet. Courtney felt bad that she'd given away his secret crush, but keeping herself and her friends safe was more important than massaging his feelings.

"We don't have time for this junior high school crap," Reyna said, shooting daggers at Courtney with her eyes. "We need to keep going. If you feel like turning back, then do it, okay? The rest of us can go on without you."

"No, I'm going with you," Courtney said, "because I don't want you to do anything stupid. You just act without thinking sometimes." Reyna was so stubborn, she was ignoring the advice J.G. was giving them—and J.G. was the only one who actually knew Leonard and what the man was capable of.

J.G. had been crouching down in the snow to conserve energy, and now he stood up slowly. "If we're going to keep walking, we better do it fast. If Leonard's around, I don't want to be out here when it gets dark, and neither do you."

"Fine," Reyna said. "I'm not the one holding us up."

Led by J.G., they left the eerie cross behind and started to walk again. They'd only gone a few paces when J.G. said, "Wait. I need to see inside the van."

"Why?" Reyna asked. "You already know what it looks like."

"Maybe I can get the CB working."

"We tried that."

"I have a knack for these things," J.G. replied.

Although Courtney wasn't looking forward to seeing the frozen corpse of the guard again, if J.G. could get the radio working, they could be off this desolate road and back in civilization within the hour. Courtney could almost feel the imagined warmth flowing through her veins.

"It's worth a try," she conceded. "A really quick try."

They walked over to the van, which was now buried even deeper in snow, as though it was becoming a permanent part of the landscape. The four of them reached the vehicle at roughly the same moment, but Reyna was the first to peer through one of the windows.

"Oh God, this is too creepy," she declared.

Courtney felt the fine hairs on the back of her neck begin to stand up as she leaned forward and looked inside. The front seat of the van was empty, except for a light covering of snow. The guard's body was gone.

X

"I thought you said—" Jeremy began, but Reyna cut him off.

"Yes, there was a body. The driver."

"He's gone," Courtney said. She turned her head and saw that J.G. was looking at her. There was something odd in his eyes, a strange, hard glint that she didn't like. "Leonard took him," Courtney said to J.G., partly just to say something so he wouldn't keep staring at her. "Didn't he?"

"I would guess so."

"It could have been one of the others," Jeremy pointed out.

"No, they're long gone," J.G. replied. "It was Leonard. I just know."

"If he did it, I don't suppose there's any logical reason,

is there?" Reyna asked. "That would be expecting too much."

"I told you. Psychopaths aren't logical."

"Maybe he did it to cover up the murder," Courtney said, although with blood still all over the seats, that seemed unlikely.

"You sure the guy was really dead?" Jeremy asked.

"He didn't get up and walk away on his own, that's for certain."

J.G. pushed himself off from the van and moved around to the other side. Courtney tracked him with her eyes. She was still afraid he might try to run if he got the chance. She knew it was probably only the handcuffs that kept him from ditching them and disappearing into town on his own.

"Over here," he called out, as Courtney and the others went after him. "There're tracks in the snow."

Courtney reached the other side of the van and followed J.G.'s gaze. Although the snow had obliterated much of the trail, she could see traces of where some large object had been dragged out of the van and into the woods. Human shoeprints ran alongside it. She followed the trail with her eyes, wondering where it ended.

"Could an animal have done this?" Jeremy asked. "I mean, dragged the body out of the van?"

Reyna broke the ensuing silence. "Do animals wear shoes?"

Jeremy was taken aback. "I'm just saying, you heard noises last night and thought some animal was out here.

A panther or a mountain lion. Maybe a wolf . . ." His words trailed away. "I dunno, I guess you're right."

"I told you who did this. It's Leonard Bell," J.G. said.

Courtney surveyed the dismal landscape, thinking that Leonard, or whoever had taken the body, could explode out of the trees at any moment. And if Leonard had the rifle, they would all become his prisoners, assuming he wanted to keep them alive.

Courtney felt more afraid now than she had at any point since waking up on the road after the accident. The fear pressed down on her chest, like a real, physical sensation. *First the blizzard, then the accident, then J.G., and now this.* Courtney felt trapped in a downward spiral that she couldn't control.

J.G. pushed his hands out from under his jacket, took off his cap, and rubbed his short, bristly hair. The chain linking the cuffs together clattered with every movement. "Leonard took the body off into the forest, and then he came back and dug that cross," he said.

"Why would he do that?" Courtney found the courage to ask.

J.G. sighed. "Maybe he decided to cover up the murder after all. If he buries the body out here, there's a good chance no one'll find it till spring." J.G. paused. "Or maybe he wants the body for some other sick reason."

Courtney realized that J.G. sounded frightened of Leonard, just as they were frightened of J.G. himself. In a way, it made J.G. seem more human.

Reyna was squinting into the woods, but the snow

made everything impenetrable. "If he knows we're out here, and wanted us to find the cross and the van, then we're in trouble," she said. "That means he's predicting our movements."

"Maybe he thinks we'll follow his trail," Courtney conjectured, "and look for the body. But there's no way we should do that. We need to get to town as soon as possible if we're not going back to the SUV."

J.G. put his cap back on, pulling it down low over his eyes. "We still need to try the CB," he reminded them. Courtney wondered what he was thinking and feeling, if he was as cold, hungry, and tired as they were. She imagined he must be, but perhaps prison had inured him to those feelings.

Courtney watched as he went over to the window and looked inside. She sensed that he didn't want to get too close to anything, that he didn't want to incriminate himself. She feared that the radio wouldn't work, and despite J.G.'s efforts, it didn't. She guessed that either Leonard, or the storm, had done some irrevocable harm to it.

Reyna took out a Gatorade bottle and passed it around. The liquid was cold, but at least it helped quench Courtney's thirst. It seemed like torture to be so thirsty when they were surrounded by snow. Yet Courtney knew they could easily get hypothermia if they ate the snow without letting it melt first.

The group eventually began moving again, away from the van and in the direction of the town. Courtney knew they'd only traveled roughly a mile, which meant they had twelve more to go. Walking on the road was probably the easy part. She didn't want to think about what it would be like when they had to hike into the forest and cut across the mountain to the town.

Courtney and the group made slow progress through the snow, falling naturally into a single-file line. J.G. was at the front, leading the way, followed by Reyna, then Courtney, and then Jeremy right behind her with the hatchet. They were too exhausted to talk, so there was plenty of time to think. Now that it was morning, Courtney knew that her parents would soon be heading toward a state of total hysteria. They hadn't wanted her to go on the ski trip to begin with. Her mom was always worried that Courtney would fall and break a bone whenever she went skiing. She'd tried to entice Courtney into staying home, but as usual, Courtney hadn't paid her mother much attention.

I guess I should have listened this time, she thought dully. But skiing was something she loved, and she didn't want it taken away from her. When she was skiing, she felt free. It was one of the few times she didn't feel any degree of self-consciousness. She could stop overanalyzing things for a moment and just relax into gliding smoothly down the slope.

Courtney knew her parents had reason to be nervous, though. She had grown up an only child, but when she was very young, she'd had an older brother named Elliot. He had died of a blood infection when he was nine, and she was only two years old. She didn't remember him at all, not even a little bit, and her parents kept no pictures of him on display. Yet sometimes she could tell her mom was thinking about him, from a certain kind of distant look she got in her eyes.

Courtney rarely thought about her dead brother because it made her feel too sad for her parents, and sometimes for herself. She'd tried to write an essay about him for school once, but had given up because it made her cry too much. She just hoped she'd get out of the wilderness soon, so her parents wouldn't be too terrified or sad about her.

It took Courtney and the others about three hours to get less than two miles from the van. These distances were just rough estimates, based mainly on J.G.'s knowledge of the area. They took a break from their harrowing odyssey, tossing down their packs and huddling at the side of the road. There, they were partially protected from the cold winds by the mountainous snowdrifts. Only ten more miles to go, Courtney thought. It sounded impossible.

As they rested their aching bodies, Courtney thought she heard something echo faintly through the trees. She grabbed Reyna's arm and gestured for everyone to stop moving.

"Listen," she said. "Hear that?"

"No. What?" Reyna asked.

They were all looking at Courtney, J.G.'s eyes boring holes into her. "I thought I heard a weird noise, like we heard last night. Something"—she groped for the right word—"baying." The sound had been brief and high-pitched, like a hyena.

"Could it be a siren?" Jeremy asked. "Maybe it's the police."

Courtney envied his optimism, but she knew that he was indulging in wishful thinking. "As if."

J.G. tilted his head to one side, concentrating. Courtney brushed some hair away from her face with a gloved hand. She wondered if she'd just been imagining things; in fact, she hoped that was the case. They didn't need anything else to worry about.

After they had waited there for another minute or two without hearing anything, Reyna turned to the prisoner. "What kinds of animals live out here? You should know, right?"

"Wolves are a possibility. They're rare in Colorado, but I've seen them in these parts before."

"Would they be a danger to us?"

J.G. shrugged. "Depends if they're hungry enough. And if it's a lone wolf, or if it's a pack."

Courtney took solace in the fact he didn't seem too scared, not in the same way he was about Leonard. "There are four of us," Courtney said. "We have the hatchet. The wolves will probably run away from us."

"Possibly," J.G. agreed.

"But you don't know for sure," Jeremy pressed. "Do you?"

"No, I don't," J.G. said, standing up. "But a man without doubt is a man without wisdom, eh?"

No one knew what to say in response to that one.

Courtney stood up too, stretching her arms, and Reyna did the same. "We better keep walking," she said.

Jeremy pushed himself up into a standing position with the help of a snowbank.

They began moving again, but they went slower, and Courtney noticed they all stuck closer together, even J.G.

"If it's a wolf pack, we need a plan," Courtney said as they walked. She was hoping J.G. would weigh in with some brilliant idea, but he didn't say a word.

"Wolves are scared of fire," Reyna pointed out. "And we have matches in one of the backpacks. We can set something on fire and stave them off."

Courtney didn't want to remind Reyna how much trouble they'd had getting a decent fire going back at the SUV. "What if we don't have time for that? If we see a wolf, should we run?" She knew it might be a stupid question, but she wanted an answer.

"Never run from a wolf," J.G. said. "You always have to stand your ground."

"But that's easier said than done," Courtney pointed out. "If a wolf comes at me, I'm not just going to wait around and let it eat me."

"Wolves can sense fear," J.G. said, his eyes fixed straight ahead as he walked. "Wolves are pack minded, like people. If we stand our ground, they'll back down. We're taller, bigger. We can make more noise. We can show them who's dominant."

Alex McAulay

"What if it's not wolves?" Jeremy asked, between ragged breaths. "What if it's a mountain lion, or a bear or something?"

"Same logic applies," J.G. said. "Believe me, we'll be lucky if we only encounter natural wildlife out here."

In the silence, broken only by the noise of their feet trudging through the snow, Courtney listened for more animal noises. None came. She felt somewhat reassured by J.G.'s words, although she knew if a large predator burst out of the forest, she would definitely start running.

"So what happens if Leonard comes?" Reyna asked. "Will fire keep him away too?"

J.G. didn't respond to Reyna's sarcasm. Instead, he said something that made the fear well up inside Courtney again. "I've been having this feeling lately that maybe he's watching us."

Courtney and Reyna exchanged glances. "When were you going to mention that?" Reyna asked.

"I wasn't, until you asked," J.G. countered. "But the feeling keeps growing stronger. It's just a hunch, but I'm worried he might be in the forest right now, following us and keeping pace. It'd be slow going in the brush, but there's four of us, so he can probably move fast enough to keep up." He looked at Courtney. "It's possible those noises could be coming from him." He said the information grudgingly, as though he hadn't wanted to admit his fears. "Maybe to scare us."

To be honest, Courtney hadn't really believed that

those peculiar keening sounds—which had been so distinctly animalistic in nature—could have come from a person. But then again, she didn't know Leonard. She tried to imagine what Leonard would be like, how it would feel to see him lumbering out onto the road, clutching a rifle. She pictured him as some kind of deformed monster, straight out of *The Hills Have Eyes.* She shuddered.

Reyna coughed a few times into her gloved hand, as though she were getting a cold. When she recovered, she said to J.G., "Obviously something's out there. We just have to be careful either way."

J.G. was unimpressed. "Like your friend told me earlier, that's easier said than done."

Courtney looked at her watch. It was almost one o'clock already, which meant it would be pitch-dark in just five hours. She knew they still had a very long way to walk. "If we don't hurry, we're going to be outside when night comes." She knew that no one wanted that. It would be intolerable to spend another night in the snow, this time without any shelter.

"Then let's quit stalling," Reyna said. "C'mon." She started wading faster through the snow, as though challenging the others to keep up. Courtney and Jeremy hobbled along after her, with J.G. at their side.

"I need a cigarette," Jeremy muttered, but no one could help, because none of them smoked except him.

"You should have bummed some off Harris," Courtney said.

"Too late now."

Courtney fervently hoped they would reach the town before nightfall, but in her heart, she thought it was unlikely. She knew they wouldn't be able to keep up this pace for long without getting tired out. We'll make it, she told herself, tumbling the words over in her mind like a mantra. *No matter what.* But she knew it was probably a lie.

XI

our hours later, Courtney and her three companions had traveled roughly four more miles, putting their total at seven. It was far, Courtney knew, but not far enough. There was no question of walking much longer, and it wasn't just because it was getting darker and colder by the second. It was because their bodies were giving out.

Courtney's thigh and calf muscles had been cramping in painful spasms for the last half hour. She imagined this must be what it felt like to complete some grueling triathlon. She wished she was in better shape, but she'd never been much of an athlete except for skiing. Every step now required great care and precision. Without concentrating on her movements, she feared she'd just fall into the snow and collapse.

She could tell Reyna and Jeremy were suffering too. Reyna kept coughing, and Jeremy's hands hadn't left his ribs for the last hour. He'd also developed a limp somewhere along the way.

Only J.G. seemed to have any remaining energy, although Courtney wondered if he was faking it. At one point, she'd noticed the handcuffs had rubbed bleeding sores on both of his wrists. He didn't complain or even mention it. It was as though he existed in a realm beyond physical pain.

Despite her agony, Courtney didn't want to be the first person to say she thought they should stop walking. It was partly because she didn't want to let Melanie and the others down, but it was also because she didn't want to let herself down. She didn't want to feel like the weak link, the one who couldn't hack it. She'd always wondered how she would act in a crisis, and here was a genuine—if unwanted—chance to find out what she was made of. She knew she had a tendency to give up on things when they got too hard, at least according to her parents and her teachers, but right now, she couldn't give up.

I'm going to keep pushing ahead until someone else says otherwise, she told herself, taking another painful step forward. Courtney didn't know if it was brave of her, or just stupid. Out here, the line between those distinctions had become blurred.

To her relief, just a few minutes later, Jeremy faltered and stumbled down to one knee. Courtney took it as her cue to stop too, as did Reyna and J.G.

"You okay?" Reyna asked Jeremy, trying to help him up.

"I'm fine." He sounded pissed off.

"You don't look fine," Reyna said. In the gathering darkness, Courtney could see the concern on her face. J.G. watched the scene impassively.

Jeremy staggered up again. "I'll be all right. Don't worry about me." It sounded like he was trying to be macho, but failing. Courtney was worried about him. He'd been acting a little strangely on and off since the accident, like he was suffering from shell shock or something.

Courtney was afraid that he'd try to start walking again, so she said, "Honestly, I can't take much more of this either. My legs feel like Jell-O. We have to stop and rest, or I'm going to pass out."

Jeremy shot her a look of gratitude.

"I'm tired too," Reyna agreed, "but we're only six miles away . . ."

"It's taken us all day to go seven miles," J.G. said. "It's getting too dark to find the way now, and we're tired. That's when people make mistakes. We need to set up camp for the night."

"Will we survive a night out here?" Courtney asked. "In case you haven't noticed, we don't have tents or anything."

"We'll find a slope and dig ourselves into the snow," J.G. said, slipping his hands out and pointing toward the trees. Courtney felt slightly giddy with fatigue, and she thought it was grimly funny he had to use both hands to point because of the cuffs. "We'll make a snow cave like the Eskimos do. Our body heat will keep us alive."

"We can start a fire too—" Reyna began, but J.G. cut her off instantly.

"No fires. They'll give us away if Leonard's watching."

"But what about wolves?" Courtney asked, worried. "We need a fire to keep them away."

"I'd rather face ten packs of wolves than Leonard Bell," J.G. replied. "The worst a wolf can do is rip out your throat."

"It can't get much worse than that," Jeremy pointed out. Courtney saw that bits of ice had formed at the edges of his sideburns. She knew it wouldn't be long until frostbite started affecting them all. She was surprised it hadn't happened already.

Then she had an awful thought: what if it had, and she just hadn't noticed? She wiggled her toes madly and clenched her hands into fists. She could feel everything, albeit barely, so she guessed she was okay for the moment.

"I've been in tougher spots than this one," J.G. was telling Jeremy, and it didn't sound like an idle boast. "If we stay smart, we'll stay safe."

It was strange to hear what amounted to a pep talk coming out of J.G., but there it was.

"Then let's stay here for the night," Reyna decreed. "We'll camp off the road until morning, and we'll start walking again when the sun comes up."

Courtney agreed, but she was thinking that it was going to be a very long, painful night for all of them.

The ragged group of four walked slowly over to the edge of the road, where the snow was so thick it nearly reached Courtney's head.

"Better start digging," J.G. said. "Jeremy, you can finally put that hatchet to use."

He nodded.

"What do the rest of us use to dig?" Courtney asked, fearing she knew the answer.

"Your hands," J.G. confirmed. Then he paused for a moment. "You know, this really would be easier if you'd get these cuffs off me. I feel like a chained monkey."

There was an uneasy silence, interrupted by the distant cracking sounds of branches giving way under the weight of the snow.

"We can't do that," Reyna said softly. "Please stop asking."

"I'm sorry," Courtney added. She was surprised to realize that somewhere along the way she'd stopped thinking of J.G. as a threat. The possibility of Leonard, and the wolves, had chased away some of her initial fear of the prisoner, even if she still didn't completely trust him.

J.G. looked around in the twilight gloom, fixing each of them in turn with his eyes. Courtney wanted to look away, but she didn't. "So it's like that," he said. "And after all we've been through together." He sounded almost sarcastic. "How sad."

"Look, we don't have any way to free you, even if we wanted to," Courtney said.

"Sure you do. The hatchet."

"That wouldn't break the chain," Reyna pointed out.

"With enough blows it would." J.G. looked around. "We find a rock, I pull the chain tight across it, and then Jeremy lets loose. The whole thing might take a while, but it'd give after enough hits. It's just metal."

No one looked enthused about his plan.

"How can I prove myself to you?" he asked, sounding frustrated. "What do you want from me? I'm helping you, aren't I? Without me, you'd be lost. I'm trying to get us to safety, but you're acting too stupid and prejudiced to see that clearly."

"Prejudiced?" Reyna asked. Her tone was suddenly ice-cold, and Courtney knew why. By using that word, he had raised an issue that none of them had confronted him on yet. Reyna took a step toward J.G. in anger. "Who's the one with the racist tattoos, huh? That's right, I saw the Aryan Nation tattoo on your shoulder. You probably have worse ones too, so don't talk to me about prejudice."

In a way, Courtney was surprised that Reyna hadn't brought up the tattoos earlier. While Courtney found them offensive and disturbing, she guessed they were even more personally abhorrent to Reyna, whose grandparents had originally come to America from Haiti. With her dark skin, Reyna was a reflection of her heritage, and Courtney knew she did not take racist crap from anyone.

"Is that what's scaring you?" J.G. asked, sounding surprised. "My tattoos? I got them because I had to. Everyone belongs to a gang in prison, that's the way it works. Everyone. The Latins, the Aryans, the homies—" He was starting to get loud. "I'm white. My skin is white. There was only one option open to me, unless I wanted to bend over and be someone's bitch. In prison, you do whatever it takes to survive . . . just like out here in this wasteland. Tattoos are nothing but ink on my skin. And if that ink saves my life, then it's worth it, understand?"

"No," Reyna hissed back. "Because I wouldn't get tattoos like that even if my life was at stake. I wouldn't betray the values I believe in."

"You're lucky. You'll probably never have to make that choice. Your parents have money, I can tell. If you ever got into trouble with the police, they could afford a good lawyer for you." He paused. "Besides, you never know what you'll do unless you have to. Everyone thinks they're a hero, but when the chips are down, no one really is. Underneath, everyone is scared. No matter what, people want to save their own skin."

"You defiled yours," Reyna told him.

J.G.'s eyes found hers. "But I'm alive, aren't I?" He held up his handcuffs. "Even if I'm in chains."

Courtney was afraid the argument would keep escalating, so she said to him, "Listen, if you don't stop this, it won't matter, because we'll all be dead. Let's just start digging and get out of the cold, okay?"

"Yeah," Jeremy said. He looked weak, and was swaying a little from side to side. "I need to sit down."

"Fine," J.G. said, relenting in frustration. "Keep my cuffs on. It doesn't matter anyway."

"Good," Courtney said, but she felt disturbed by J.G.'s outburst. It was like he didn't even realize his crazy tattoos were so hateful and repellent.

Courtney and the group walked to where the snowfall was deepest, put their packs down on the snow, and began to carve a large opening in the side of the snowbank. In some ways, it was easier than Courtney had expected. The soft snow gave way without much force, and the hole grew larger with every passing moment. All four of them were working on it, grunting and swearing, trying to burrow into the snow and make a place where they could escape the harsh elements. Courtney, Reyna, and Jeremy all took turns swinging the hatchet to break up the snow. Courtney knew the night was going to be brutal, but she hoped they could at least get some rest until morning. She also knew it would be tense inside the snow cave, because Reyna wouldn't even look at J.G. anymore.

It took over an hour until the cave was complete. By then, they were seeing only by the light of the moon, which poked through thin strips of clouds in the night sky. It was no longer snowing, but the wind had picked up and was whipping the fallen snow around. Courtney noted it was much colder at night, and the pain was hard to endure. She was proud of their cave, though.

The hole went deep into the snowbank, back at least six feet or more. They had dug downward and then carved out some of the snow above them and on either side, which meant the hole was about five feet in height and width. There would barely be room for their four bodies inside it. Courtney wished they could have made it even larger, but they were too tired and cold to continue digging. Besides, the tighter the space, the warmer it would be.

J.G. instructed them on how to pack the walls firmly and make it so that the snow cave wouldn't collapse.

"Did you learn this stuff in the army?" Jeremy asked at one point, as they worked.

"No. From TV," J.G. admitted. "The Discovery Channel. In jail, you watch a lot of TV. There's not much else to do."

"Let's hope it holds up," Courtney said, wishing J.G. had just lied and told them he was a snow expert or something. She didn't want to get buried and smothered during the night.

"We'll be safer in there than out here," J.G. told her. "I know that much."

Courtney and the others took their packs and the hatchet into their homemade refuge, shoving snow in front of the opening, so they were mostly cut off from the outside world except for a tiny breathing hole.

Courtney thought that the good thing about their cave was that it was unlikely Leonard or any dangerous animal would find them in it. The bad thing was that they

133

were all crammed together in a tiny, uncomfortable space that was freezing cold and dark. Droplets of water, heated by their bodies, kept falling down on them. Courtney pressed herself tighter against the icy wall, partly to put more space between herself and J.G. He was sitting to her left, with Jeremy to her right, and Reyna slightly in front of them.

"Feels like being back in prison," J.G. muttered at one point, and Courtney thought it was one of the few times she'd heard him say anything resembling a joke. She'd noticed he rarely smiled—at least not genuinely—and wondered if he'd always been that way or if it was a trait he'd picked up in prison. He remained a total mystery to her, rarely talking unless he had something specific to say. She wished she knew more about him, but didn't want to ask any personal questions in case the answers scared her.

"It's so cold," Jeremy said, rubbing his arms back and forth to warm them up. "Will this cave thing really work?"

"It better," Reyna replied, shivering. And then she added bluntly, "Or else we're going to freeze to death."

Courtney refused to think about that possibility. She wished Reyna hadn't even given voice to it. "Dying isn't an option," she said. "Okay?"

"If you say so," Reyna replied. Since her argument with J.G., she'd been in a bad mood. Courtney felt alone, like she was in some sort of space capsule, stranded and separated from the rest of the world. She dug in the pack and passed around the remainder of the

Gatorade and the energy bars, thinking it might help them feel better.

"We'll be fine," J.G. said eventually, tilting his head back on the side of the cave, using an icy shelf like a bizarre pillow. "Snow caves have worked for centuries for the Eskimos. If they could bear it for hundreds of years, we can bear it for one night." He seemed calmer now that they were out of the snow. "I'm going to get some shut-eye, if you don't mind."

"How the hell can you sleep in a place like this?" Jeremy asked above the sound of the wind outside.

As he closed his eyes, J.G. added, "You'd be surprised how quickly people can adapt to extreme circumstances."

"Maybe." Jeremy didn't sound convinced.

Courtney yearned to stretch out her aching legs and massage the muscles, but there was no room. And I thought the SUV was cramped, she mused. This was far worse. She wondered how Melanie and Harris were faring and hoped they were doing okay. She was so exhausted, she felt like she was beyond sleep, but it came to her in minutes.

Courtney fell directly into strange dreams, nightmarish images of the past twenty-four hours washing over her. She would wake up with a sudden lurch, thinking she was still in the SUV, safely on her way home to Denver. Then reality would creep back in and she'd remember what had happened to her. It felt unbelievable the way her life had taken such an unexpected turn.

At one point she woke up and everyone else seemed to be sleeping, or at least barely conscious. Reyna had fallen sideways and was slumped against Jeremy's shoulder. He hadn't even noticed, because he was sleeping deepest of them all, his slow, deep breaths amplified by the walls of snow and ice. She wondered if he'd be mad at her when they got back home for revealing that he liked Reyna. She hoped that he wouldn't be, but she felt a little guilty about it. She had enough self-awareness to know she'd partly done it because she was jealous he didn't like her, at least not in that way. Yet she valued their friendship and didn't want to damage it.

Courtney wanted daylight to come soon. She vowed to stay awake until then, so she could see the first hint of light outside the front of their cave, but restless sleep claimed her again. The intense cold made her feel drugged. At a later point in the night she thought she heard a distant crash from somewhere in the forest, and she curled up even tighter, afraid it was a pack of wolves, or worse. But the noise didn't come again.

When she woke up again, struggling to put her hazy thoughts in order, it was finally morning. As she tried to open her eyes and get her arms and legs to come alive, she realized that the snow cave felt different somehow. Jeremy was still snoring, and things seemed peaceful, so it took her disoriented mind a second to realize exactly what was wrong.

Then, with a burst of fear, she understood. There was way too much room in the cave, too much empty space.

Courtney started forward in horror, trying to claw her way out of the front of the cave, hoping there was some kind of mistake. It was only when she got outside, in the stark, white, snow-covered world, that she knew for sure something terrible had happened during the night. She stood there, gazing around, barely able to feel her numb body, except for the prickling sensation of fear down the back of her neck.

Reyna was gone, and so was J.G.

And there was no trace of either of them.

XII

Courtney turned back to the snow cave and plunged through the opening, shouting for Jeremy. "Get up!" she yelled, grabbing at the front of his jacket. "Get the fuck up!"

He opened his bleary eyes. "Courtney?" he asked, sounding dazed.

"Get up, Jer! Something's happened!"

Hearing the urgency in her words, he forced his body upward, grappling his way out of their burrow and into the gray daylight. He crouched down on all fours outside for a moment, as though he felt light-headed, before he finally stood all the way up, rubbing his side.

Courtney gestured for him to look around, fighting tears. "Reyna's gone, and so is J.G.," she told him.

Jeremy's eyes widened. "Oh my God," he said, looking back and forth.

Courtney was desperately scrutinizing the landscape for any sign of her friend or the prisoner. "It could be nothing," she said, the words ringing false in her ears. "Maybe they woke up before us and went to go get something . . ."

"He took her," Jeremy said. His face was turning from pale white to deep red as he grew more upset. "Jesus fucking Christ! J.G. took her."

Courtney was thinking the same thing, because she couldn't help it, but she told herself to remain calm and try to think through all the possibilities. "We don't know that yet," she said. But at the same time, her heart was pounding wildly in her chest. *Why would J.G. take Reyna?* It didn't make any sense. Where would he take her? There was nowhere to go.

"I knew we couldn't trust him!" Jeremy started raving, stumbling in a semicircle through the snow. "Motherfucker!"

"Please, Jeremy," Courtney begged. "Stay calm for me. Don't lose it."

Jeremy pointed at her, jabbing his finger angrily at her chest. "I'm not the one who's lost it! That freak is the one who's crazy. Not me!"

Courtney could tell that Jeremy's mind was crumbling under the weight of fear and panic, and she frantically tried to think of a way to keep him sane. "Jeremy, it's just us," she said. "Just me and you right now. We have to put our heads together and figure out what's happened. We need to find—"

Jeremy swung his body toward her, his face contorted with confused rage. "If J.G. hurts Reyna, I'm going to fucking kill him!" he ranted. "He'll be sorry he ever met us. We should have left him to die." He looked at Courtney, and she was surprised to see a look of accusation in his eyes. "Why didn't we leave him out there? Why'd you want to bring him inside?"

"Stop it," Courtney said. "If we hadn't rescued him, it would have been murder." She exhaled deeply, trying to regain her equilibrium. "We don't know that J.G. did anything yet. We have to focus and find him and Reyna. Without him, we don't know where we're going. We're completely lost on this road."

Her words seemed to be having some effect, but it was limited. When Jeremy spoke again, his voice was softer, but his tone remained angry. "Just remember what I said. If he hurt Reyna, he's a dead man."

Courtney thought those words sounded so incongruous coming out of Jeremy's mouth. She remembered Reyna's earlier comment about Jeremy—*he's so emo*—and wondered what Reyna would make of him now. Courtney missed the old Jeremy, the one she could count on, the one who made her laugh. But that Jeremy had been partially absent since the car accident, as though something were slowly eating away at him.

Jeremy muttered a few more epithets and finally fell

silent. Courtney didn't want to point out that his tantrum had probably cost them crucial minutes.

"Let's think," she pressed him. "Which way would they go? Do you see any footprints?" She hadn't noticed any herself, but thought that giving Jeremy a task would help keep him calm. She knew she had to stay single-minded on finding Reyna and J.G., and not get distracted.

Jeremy looked around. "Nothing."

"Keep looking," she said, but the snow had covered any indication of human footsteps. It must have snowed more during the night, she thought.

Courtney realized it was possible that J.G. and Reyna might have left several hours ago. She cursed herself for not waking up, and wondered how she hadn't heard the two of them leave. Assuming J.G. had taken Reyna by force, she doubted Reyna would have been quiet about it. Reyna wasn't that kind of girl. *Unless maybe J.G. had a weapon.*

"The hatchet," Courtney said suddenly, her heart sinking. "Check the cave."

Jeremy didn't ask why. He walked over to the remains of their snow cave, wearing a look of helpless desperation. Courtney knew that both she and Jeremy expected the hatchet to be gone, and probably their backpacks too, so it was a surprise when they saw everything was still there. Courtney and Jeremy looked at each other.

"It doesn't mean anything," Jeremy said, staring down at the hatchet.

"I know." But to Courtney it was a sign that things could have been worse.

"What are we going to do, Court?" Jeremy asked her. He bent down and picked up the hatchet, turning it over in his hand.

Just as she was about to speak, her mind struggling to figure out a solution, she heard the unmistakable sound of something moving through the pine forest. Courtney heard the icy crust beneath the snow crackling and giving way. She spun around, and so did Jeremy, just as the sound resolved into footsteps.

To their shock, J.G. came shambling out of the forest about fifty feet to their right, heading straight toward them.

"You!" Jeremy yelled. In a reflex motion he raised his hand, still grasping the hatchet.

J.G. looked a little confused, but he didn't stop walking. His hands were still cuffed, and he looked weary, with mussed-up hair like he'd woken not too long ago himself. There were no obvious signs that he'd done anything to Reyna: no blood on his clothes or hands, nothing suspicious at all.

Courtney was starting to think that maybe he didn't have anything to do with Reyna's disappearance. It was partly based on how he looked, and partly based on gut instinct. *But then, where was Reyna?*

Jeremy, however, was blinded by his fury, and didn't think to ask any questions. He'd started heading toward J.G., the hatchet still raised like he meant to decapitate the prisoner.

"Stop!" Courtney yelled, hoping to avert a disaster, but it had no effect. Jeremy kept walking.

"What the fuck did you do to her?" he screamed at a puzzled-looking J.G.

"What?" J.G. yelled back. He'd slowed his pace now, realizing that something was wrong.

"Reyna's missing!" Courtney yelled out, rushing up behind Jeremy but being careful not to get too close in case he flipped out and started swinging the hatchet.

J.G. stopped as Jeremy grew nearer.

"You did something to Reyna, I know it," Jeremy told him. "Where did you take her?"

"I don't know what you're talking about," J.G. replied warily. "When I got up, she wasn't in the snow cave. I assumed she had to go take a crap or something. That's what I was doing."

"I don't believe you!" Jeremy yelled.

J.G. looked irritated. "Did you want me to bring back a sample?"

Jeremy practically exploded in rage. "Now you're making jokes?!"

"Calm down—" Courtney said, but Jeremy turned on her and snarled. "Keep out of this, bitch!" Shocked, Courtney took a step back. She felt like she'd been slapped across the face. Never in her life did she think Jeremy would say something like that to her. She fought back a surge of hot tears.

J.G. held out his still-shackled hands to Jeremy. "Believe me, I was taking a crap, and it's not so easy to wipe with these cuffs on. Why the hell would I hurt your friend? I want to get out of this place just like you, before we freeze or get shot."

"No," Jeremy said, shaking his head. "You're scum, I know it. You hurt her." He held the weapon high. "Where are your footprints?"

"I covered them as I walked, or tried to, so they wouldn't be visible to Leonard. I assumed Reyna did the same thing, if she was smart."

Courtney took a tentative step forward again from behind Jeremy, still recovering from the surprise of his insult. "Jeremy, put that thing down so we can talk. J.G.'s here now. We can all work together to find Reyna. Just put the hatchet down."

Jeremy ignored her. "Tell me the truth, or I'm going to fuck you up," he said to the prisoner.

J.G. looked like he was bored with Jeremy's posturing. "Listen, even with cuffs on, you're probably no match for me," he said tiredly. "I bet I could take that hatchet away from you and ram it up your ass, blade first, before you could say Uncle Sam. But do you really want me to do that to you?"

Jeremy didn't reply; he just continued his slow approach. He was now circling J.G. like a predator. There was time and space for J.G. to run, but the prisoner stood his ground. Courtney didn't know what was wrong with Jeremy. It was as though all the stress had short-circuited some vital section of his brain.

"Jeremy, cut it out!" Courtney yelled at him, sensing

that he was about to attack. "This doesn't help us find Reyna!"

A moment after the words left her mouth, Jeremy lunged at the prisoner. J.G. saw the assault coming and he crouched down, pulling his head inward and pushing his shoulders out, like a linebacker. Jeremy ran forward with the hatchet upraised. Courtney didn't know if he had gone flat-out insane and was trying to kill J.G., but it looked like that to her. She wanted to glance away, but her eyes were held tight by the terrifying spectacle as she started screaming.

Just as Jeremy reached J.G., the prisoner moved sideways with surprising speed, and kicked at one of his legs. Jeremy got caught directly in the kneecap, and fell flailing into the snow, dropping the hatchet in agony. J.G. lost his balance too, and started crawling away from his assailant. He tried to get to his feet, but was having trouble because of the cuffs, so Jeremy managed to stagger upright first, clutching his knee. He appeared to have forgotten about the hatchet in his eagerness for violence, because he flung himself on J.G. without the weapon, tackling him full force. Their bodies collided, with him on top, and he began hitting J.G. in the head, fists and snow flying in a blur.

Despite her fear, Courtney saw an opportunity. She raced in, avoiding the two of them, and managed to snatch up the hatchet. It was cold and heavy, and she held it in both hands. She retreated to a safe distance, clutching the handle. She felt as though getting it was some kind of victory, that she'd reduced the chances for violence and killing. Yet when she looked back at Jeremy, he was still on top, and still pummeling the hapless prisoner. With his hands shackled, J.G. couldn't put up much of a fight, even though he bucked and kicked with his legs.

Courtney knew the two guys weren't thinking anymore. If one or both of them got injured, it would jeopardize their chances of reaching the town, and put all their lives in danger.

"Stop acting crazy!" she shouted at them, brandishing the hatchet. "Think about Reyna! Think about yourselves!"

Either her words had some effect, or Jeremy just got tired, because he finally rolled sideways, off J.G. and into the deep snow. It took Courtney a moment to realize that Jeremy was sobbing as his chest heaved for breath.

J.G. rolled up in a ball, still trying to protect his battered face with his hands. She could see bright red blood on the snow, spattered across its immaculate surface.

"Oh God!" Jeremy wept, as though he were having a complete breakdown. In comparison, J.G. was totally silent.

Courtney didn't know what to do. She took a few steps closer to the two of them, holding the hatchet out in front of her. "Jer?" she asked softly.

"Leave me alone," he replied, the words coming out as a low, agonized moan. She saw that there was blood on his knuckles and didn't know if it belonged to him or J.G. Whatever fury had possessed Jeremy now seemed to have leeched from his body. He continued to weep as he slumped in the snow. Courtney was shocked at what he'd done. She hadn't thought he was the kind of person who could assault someone like that.

"It's okay," she said, moving even closer, trying to placate Jeremy and also examine J.G.'s injuries. She prayed that Jeremy hadn't hurt J.G. too badly, or else it would hinder their efforts to find Reyna and get out of the wild.

"It'll never be okay again," Jeremy replied, his voice muffled by the snow.

J.G. was moving, and slowly sitting up. His nose was leaking blood and one of his eyes already appeared swollen. He saw Courtney standing over him with the hatchet, and to her surprise, he smiled. His teeth were red.

"Aren't you going to finish the job?" he asked her. Then he spat out a jet of blood and saliva into the snow next to her boot. Courtney didn't know what to say.

"I'm sorry," she told him, because it was the first thing that came into her mind, although she wasn't sure what she was apologizing for.

"I didn't hurt Reyna," J.G. told her. He picked up a handful of snow and pressed it against his face, wincing in pain. "Your friend's got the wrong idea." Courtney thought it was ironic that J.G., a convicted felon, was suddenly acting far more rationally than Jeremy. "Reyna couldn't have gotten far, not in this place," J.G. continued. He stroked his damaged face with his thin fingers and then said, "Does my nose look okay?"

Courtney nodded, even though it looked swollen and deformed.

J.G. grinned again. "You're lying." He hauled himself slowly to his feet. "It's broken." When he was all the way up, he looked down at Jeremy, who was curled up in the snow a few paces away. He shook his head. "That's a hell of a way to win a fight."

Courtney was glad that he didn't seem angry. If anything, he seemed relieved, like he'd been anticipating some kind of violent catharsis all along. "Will you help me look for Reyna?" she asked. "Please? Something bad happened to her, I know it. Why would she disappear like this?"

Courtney knew she was taking a risk, because it was still possible Jeremy was right, and J.G. really was the culprit. Yet he was cuffed, he'd just got beaten up, and she had the hatchet. If he tried anything weird, she was pretty sure she'd be able to defend herself.

J.G. wiped his hands on the leg of his jeans. "Bathroom's the only reason I can think of." He turned toward the forest. "She would have headed into the trees for that. Not that anyone's around to see us."

"But why hasn't she come back out?" Courtney remembered the animal sounds they'd heard the day before, and shuddered. "We have to go look for her. She could be hurt. Maybe something attacked her . . ."

"Maybe so."

Courtney swallowed. "Could Leonard have got her?"

"That's possible too."

They heard a noise and turned to see Jeremy getting up from the snow, brushing it off the front of his jacket. J.G. took a step away from him, seemingly concerned that Jeremy might start attacking him again. But Courtney could tell that all the fight was gone from her friend. Jeremy looked at them, his heavy gaze filled with bitterness and suspicion.

"J.G. did this," he said to Courtney.

"Look," Courtney told Jeremy, trying to keep the peace, "I don't think J.G. had anything to do with it. But if he did, then he's the only one who knows where she is. We still need his help to find—"

"I'm telling you, I have no idea where she went," J.G. interrupted. "But I'll help you look. Because then you'll believe me, and then we can get to town." He sighed. "You kids don't do anything but bitch and fuss, do you?"

Courtney turned to Jeremy. His face was still wet from his crying fit, and he was trying to dry it on his jacket sleeve.

"We'll start in the forest nearby," Courtney said. "There aren't any tracks to follow, but she's clearly not out on the road, or we'd see her."

Jeremy nodded stiffly.

"We don't have much time," Courtney added, still gripping the hatchet.

Prodded forward by Courtney's words, J.G. and

Jeremy headed slowly into the forest, all three of them calling out Reyna's name as they walked through the snow. The forest was so silent Courtney could sometimes hear the sound of her own blood pulsing through her ears. There were no birds, no squirrels. Just snow, and the occasional crack of a branch. Everything seemed deadened to her, as though the snow had erased the natural world and imposed something alien and forbidding on top of it. I'll be happy if I never see snow again after this, Courtney thought. *Not one single snowflake.*

They did not receive any response to their cries, not even an echo. Their words drifted out into the vast expanse of snow and trees. What if we don't find her? Courtney thought. *What are we going to do then?* At some point they would have to make the difficult decision of either staying there and risking their own lives, as well as Harris's and Melanie's, or plowing ahead to the town and risking Reyna's.

"Reyna, where are you?!" Courtney yelled, hoping they would never have to make that choice.

J.G. stopped and watched the forest ahead. The snow on the trees made it difficult to see very far in front of them.

"You hear something?" Courtney asked him, because he was wearing a look of intense concentration.

Slowly, he shook his head. "No. But look over there. Looks like there's a cliff or something."

"A cliff?" Courtney asked, not seeing it.

Jeremy's eyes struggled to follow her gaze.

Courtney finally saw what J.G. was talking about, some kind of steep drop-off, partially masked by the whiteness on the ground and on the trees. It was about twenty yards ahead of them. She pointed for Jeremy's benefit, relieved J.G. had seen it; otherwise they might have slipped and stumbled over the edge. "Let's check it out."

"Why the hell would Reyna come all the way out here?" Jeremy asked, agitated again. He pointed at J.G. angrily. "That bastard had something to do with this, I'm telling you. He's playing with us."

Courtney agreed it didn't sound like Reyna to walk into the forest randomly and get disoriented, but she knew accidents could happen to anyone. She also knew that out here, people's personalities could apparently change, like Jeremy calling her a bitch. "We have to go look," she said decisively, forging ahead. She started calling Reyna's name again.

Jeremy and J.G. trudged after her toward the strange precipice. Courtney glanced up as they walked, seeing the frozen branches of the trees splayed out above her like a white latticework. She could feel her heart beating in her chest when she looked back in front of her and saw the edge of the cliff approaching.

The land cut off in front of them abruptly, and then emerged again at the bottom, about fifteen feet below. From a distance, however, the snow and trees created the illusion that the land was roughly even. Courtney realized it would be very easy to make a mistake, even in the daytime, and fall over the edge.

She picked up her pace as she grew closer, feeling a sudden, urgent desire to make sure that Reyna hadn't come this way in the night.

"Be careful," she heard J.G. warn from behind as she got near the edge and peered over. The breath caught in her throat when she realized what was there, waiting for her. She turned back and saw J.G. and Jeremy approaching, still a few yards away. She wanted to tell them what she'd found, yet she felt as though all the air had been sucked out of her lungs.

"What is it?" Jeremy asked, seeing the stricken look on her face, but she still couldn't reply.

Jeremy and the prisoner reached Courtney at approximately the same tlme, looking down past her over the edge of the cliff.

Fifteen feet below them at the bottom, half buried in a pile of rubble, was Reyna's body.

XIII

Courtney put her face in Jeremy's shoulder, wanting to obliterate the vision. Yet even with her eyes shut, she could picture everything perfectly. She fought the urge to cry, because she didn't want to lose control of her emotions. Her mind churned, filled with terrible thoughts.

Did J.G. do this? she wondered. Had he thrown Reyna over the cliff? Surely Reyna would have screamed for help. It was more likely, Courtney realized, that the whole situation was some sort of accident. The cliff was difficult to discern, even in the daylight. Yet Courtney had no idea why Reyna would have wandered so far from their camp. And she feared that now they would never know, because Reyna's body looked lifeless.

When Courtney finally raised her head again, tears were leaking out the corners of her eyes. She saw that J.G. was staring at her, with his strange unblinking gaze. She wanted to rail against him in her grief and fear, but she felt too drained. She just stared back blankly.

"She's still alive, you know," J.G. said softly.

"What?" Courtney asked.

"Your friend is still alive," he repeated slowly. "We just need to get down there and help her."

"How can you tell?" Jeremy asked, looking over at J.G. and sounding as distraught as Courtney felt. "She looks"—he didn't want to say the word, but finally did—"dead."

It was true, Courtney thought. Reyna's skin was so pale that she looked completely frozen.

"I told you, I trained as a medic," J.G. explained. "I know the difference between someone who's alive and someone who's dead. You pick up that skill pretty fast." He crouched down and peered over the edge. "Look at all those rocks. I think her arm is stuck under a boulder. Maybe she triggered a small avalanche or something."

Courtney remembered the strange crashing noise she'd heard in the night, and wondered if that had been the very moment Reyna was falling off the cliff. It made her feel sad and desperate to think she'd been so unaware that her best friend was in peril.

"Reyna!" she called down to her, finally getting her voice back. "Can you hear me?" Jeremy and J.G. joined in, but they got no answer. Reyna remained still and silent in the snow. Courtney saw that her arm was indeed pinned, by a giant mass of rock that was encrusted with mud and ice. Oh Reyna, she thought, how are we going to get you out of this one?

"I'm going down to help her," J.G. announced. "Come with me—I'll need your hands."

Before Courtney could process what J.G. was doing, he took a deep breath and then jumped awkwardly right off the cliff. He landed feet first in the deep snow below, and fell forward onto his injured face. He cursed loudly as he struggled to get back on his feet, but the noises didn't stir Reyna.

Courtney knew she had to do the same thing, because there was no other quick way down. The cliff stretched out on either side of them as far as they could see. She detached herself from Jeremy's grasp and gave him the hatchet, afraid she'd accidentally impale herself if she leapt with it in her hand. She didn't really want him to have it again, but she also didn't want to toss it down to J.G. either.

Without allowing herself time to get scared, she jumped down near Reyna into thick snow. It was easier for her to jump than for J.G. because her arms weren't shackled, so she managed to stay upright when she landed. Still, it gave her a huge jolt that cracked her teeth together. She shook it off and rushed over to Reyna's side, with J.G. following a pace behind her. She heard Jeremy leap a second later, landing behind them with a loud thump, and a grunt.

Reyna wasn't moving, and there was no obvious breath visible in the cold air. The lower part of her left arm at the elbow disappeared into the shadows of the boulder. It looked like it was completely crushed beneath the mammoth rock. Courtney grabbed hold of Reyna's right arm and it felt stiff and cold to her, even through the thick winter jacket.

J.G. moved in and slid a hand under Reyna's neck, supporting it while he checked her airway and felt her neck for a pulse.

"Like I said, she's alive," he told them. "We need to get her warm. And we need to get her out from under this rock."

"Thank God," Jeremy said hesitantly, his voice trembling. He was standing right behind the two of them, watching closely.

Courtney still didn't want to get her hopes up. She never thought it would have been so difficult to tell if someone was alive or not. I have to trust J.G., she told herself. *I have to believe in his judgment.*

"Reyna," J.G. was saying, repeating her name over and over again. "Wake up, Reyna. Can you hear me?" His voice sounded detached and clinical, but oddly confident. "You need to open your eyes for me, okay? Open your eyes."

Courtney's eyes flitted over to Reyna's pinned left arm. Her hand wasn't visible at all.

"She's coming around," Jeremy suddenly said, nervous relief in his voice.

Courtney stared back down at Reyna's face just in time to see her eyes flutter open. "Rey," Courtney said, as J.G. moved in even closer to tend to her. "Jesus, I thought you were dead."

Reyna's eyes closed again. J.G. now had her good hand in his. "Can you squeeze my hand?" he asked. Reyna's fingers tightened around his, interlocking.

She licked her chapped, bloody lips. "Where am I?" With her eyes still shut, she started trying to get up.

"Don't move," J.G. instructed sharply. "You're going to be okay, but you had an accident. You fell, and you might have hit your head, or hurt your neck. Your arm is stuck underneath a rock."

"God . . ." Reyna moaned. She shifted again in the snow. J.G. let go of her hand and fought to keep her neck and head immobilized. Courtney wanted to help, but she didn't know how.

"It's important to keep still, okay, Reyna?" J.G. said, sounding just like a doctor. "I need to make sure you don't have any injuries before you start flopping around like that."

Reyna seemed to understand because she stopped moving again, although she continued moaning. J.G. kept checking her body to see where she was hurt. "We need to get her warm, and fast," he said to Courtney. He started struggling with his jacket, trying to get it all the way off to put on Reyna.

"Is she going to be all right?" Courtney asked, helping him because of the cuffs. She remembered Melanie's secret bleed, and hoped Reyna didn't have any hidden injuries.

"That depends on how well we take care of her," J.G. said. "Other than her arm, she might be okay."

Reyna moaned in pain, and Courtney's eyes teared up in sympathy for her friend. She reached down and gripped Reyna's free hand. "We're here now. You're not alone."

Following J.G.'s example, Courtney and Jeremy quickly took off additional clothing and wrapped it around Reyna, but Courtney knew it wouldn't be enough. "How are we going to get her warm out here?" she asked. "It's too cold. We have to free her arm and move her somewhere. Maybe build another snow cave nearby, or risk starting a fire."

J.G. was checking out Reyna's trapped arm, or what little they could see of it, and frowning. "I'll need your help and Jeremy's to get her loose," he said. "We need to grab her arm and yank it out of there. She'll have some broken bones in her hand and wrist, I'm sure of that." He looked down at Reyna. "Can you hear me?"

She nodded weakly.

"This is going to hurt, okay? There's no way to sugar-coat it. But at least it'll be over quickly, I promise you that."

Even in her daze, Reyna understood. Courtney saw her steeling herself for the impending pain, and was struck by Reyna's courage.

"How did this happen, Rey?" Jeremy asked from

behind them, startling her and making J.G. pause. Jeremy was pacing back and forth. Courtney guessed he was hoping Reyna would implicate J.G., but she didn't.

"I came out at night to pee . . ." Reyna muttered. "It was so stupid of me. I heard noises outside our shelter . . . animal noises, and I got scared . . . confused . . ." She took a gasping breath, saliva beading at the corners of her mouth. "Then all of a sudden I fell, and some rocks fell down with me. I passed out then, I guess . . ." Reyna twisted her head back to look at them. "Now I'm fucked."

"No, you're not, because you have us," Courtney told her.

"Grab her arm like so," J.G. said to Courtney, gesturing for her to come forward. He indicated where he wanted her to take hold of Reyna's trapped arm, on either side of her elbow. "Brace your feet for leverage." Courtney did as she was told, although it was difficult in the deep snow. J.G. pressed himself against the boulder and said, "Jeremy, get over here."

Grudgingly, Jeremy came. Courtney couldn't understand his attitude toward J.G. at this point. She wished he would just let it drop and do what was best for Reyna, and the group. It was like Jeremy didn't understand they all had to work together.

"You and me are going to push against this rock and see if we can get it off her," J.G. explained to him. "At the same time, Courtney's going to pull on her arm, okay?"

Jeremy nodded. Courtney was hoping desperately

that J.G.'s plan would work, and they could get Reyna to someplace less exposed. But the rock looked very large and heavy.

"We'll do it on the count of three," J.G. continued. He glanced at Courtney. "It's important you pull hard, but try to keep the rest of her still. If she has any internal injuries from the fall, I don't want to make them worse." He looked over at Jeremy and said, "Push as hard as you can when I say three."

"Sure," Jeremy said, not looking at him.

Reyna was murmuring something, so Courtney leaned down to hear. "Tell me."

"I'm scared," Reyna whispered back. She licked her lips. "I'm afraid of the pain. I don't want to be afraid . . . but I am."

"Don't worry," Courtney told her, trying to sound reassuring and mask her own fear. "We'll get you out of here in no time. Just hang on." The words sounded like empty platitudes to her ears, so she clutched Reyna's arm harder and added, "You've got me, Rey. I'm right here. I'm not going to let anything bad happen to you. You're my best friend, and I love you."

"Thank you," Reyna mouthed. "I don't want to be weak."

"You're not. You're the strongest person out here."

J.G. took a deep breath. One of his eyes was now entirely closed by swelling, and his nose wasn't looking so good either. "You ready?" he asked Courtney. She nodded.

Jeremy and J.G. pressed their gloved hands up against the icy boulder.

Courtney focused on Reyna's injured arm, telling herself not to screw up. Her mouth was dry from nerves and dehydration, and she felt much colder now that she had fewer clothes on. She knew they had to get Reyna free as fast as possible. She also knew they would be causing her friend a lot of pain, but it was the only way to save her.

"Let's do it," Jeremy muttered, adjusting his hands on the boulder for a better grip. "I can't take any more."

J.G. began the countdown: "One . . . two . . . and three!"

Courtney pulled with strong, steady force on Reyna's arm, as Jeremy and J.G. grunted with effort and tried to push the boulder back. Reyna began to scream in agony, but Courtney blocked out the sounds. Courtney thought she felt Reyna's arm move a little at first, but then it felt like it got stuck again. She looked over desperately at Jeremy and J.G. They were giving it everything they had, but the boulder wasn't moving at all. In a rush of despair, Courtney realized it had to be even heavier than it looked. She didn't know what to do.

"Stop! Stop!" Reyna was screaming as she writhed in the snow. She'd bitten her lip, and blood bubbled down her chin.

Courtney finally let go of Reyna, stumbling a few steps backward.

"Fuck!" Jeremy yelled, his face red with exertion. "It's

not working!" He pushed for a moment more, but it was clear nothing else was going to happen. Reyna's barrage of screams and sobs were terrible, and Courtney stood there, feeling like she'd failed.

"Enough, enough," J.G. finally said. The whole excruciating procedure hadn't lasted longer than a minute, but it felt like an hour to Courtney.

"Your idea sucks," Jeremy said to J.G in despair, as he panted. "There's no way this thing is going to budge. We need more people."

"We just need a better strategy," J.G. replied calmly. Courtney could tell he was still thinking, trying to analyze the situation. "Look for a tree branch, something we can use to stick underneath the rock for leverage, understand?"

"Of course I understand!" Jeremy snapped. "That's just what I need—a physics lecture from a drug dealer."

"We have to work together to help Reyna, don't you see that?" Courtney implored. "Don't get angry at J.G."

"That rock's not going anywhere, no matter what we do," Jeremy retorted. "It didn't even move with both of us on it. Hell, I couldn't even feel J.G. pushing. It's way too big, too heavy. Reyna's right—she's fucked. We're all fucked."

"I've still got handcuffs on," J.G. replied, sounding a little aggrieved. "You guys have a hatchet. You could get them off me with enough blows. Then maybe I could push harder—"

"Uh-uh. No way." Jeremy scowled.

Unconsciously, Courtney glanced down at Reyna, as though expecting her injured friend to deliver a verdict. But Reyna was out of commission, whimpering and crying in pain, so Courtney was on her own. "Maybe we should break the handcuffs. I mean, if it helps."

"Over my dead fucking body," Jeremy said, spitting each word out with venom. "The rock is too heavy for us. It wouldn't make a difference." His eyes were those of a stranger. "J.G. stays in handcuffs until we get to the town. That's the way it has to be."

"It's fine," J.G. broke in, before Courtney could continue the argument, as though he'd given up on Jeremy listening to reason. "Let's be smart about this. We can get the rock off her if we get better leverage, I know it." He started looking around for things to scavenge. "We just need a tree branch that's thick enough."

Courtney joined him in the search and eventually so did Jeremy. Although they were surrounded by trees, the snow made it difficult to find any fallen branches. Courtney's hands felt numb from digging in the snow, even with her gloves on. She hated the snow and the trees, detested them with a passion. This beautiful landscape was keeping her a prisoner and killing her best friend.

Courtney wasn't able to make much progress with finding anything, and Jeremy and J.G. weren't having any luck either. She doubted there was even a branch out here that would work on the boulder.

Finally J.G. stood up, breathing hard, and said, "We

can use the hatchet. We can hack a fresh branch off a tree."

Jeremy nodded in mute agreement.

Courtney went back over to Reyna's side, while J.G. and Jeremy worked at cutting down a thick pine branch. Reyna didn't look like she was doing well, her face blanched near white with cold and fear. She was semiconscious, her eyelids fluttering open and then closed again.

"Just hold on a little longer," Courtney told her, brushing the light dusting of snow off her friend's face. "We're going to get you out of here. We have a plan."

Reyna nodded her head weakly. Courtney held her hand as she heard the thwack of the hatchet; Jeremy was swinging at the branch with renewed vigor. J.G. was holding on to the end of it, trying to keep it from whipping around. Finally, Jeremy managed to cut it off the tree, the branch coming loose in J.G.'s hands. Courtney hoped that their plan would work, although to her, the boulder still seemed far too large.

"Rey, we're going to try again," she said, as Jeremy and J.G. lugged the branch over. They started digging out a place for it in the snow, trying to position it under the rock. With a great deal of effort, they finally dug it under and got it in place, so that the branch stuck out at a nearly forty-five-degree angle.

"All we do is push on the end of it. If we can raise this thing an inch, we can get her hand out," J.G. explained.

"That's a big If," Jeremy said. Obviously he was having doubts about the plan too, Courtney thought.

"Shhh," she hissed at him, only because she didn't want Reyna to be affected by his pessimism, and lose hope. She took hold of Reyna's injured arm again. "Be strong, okay?" she whispered in Reyna's ear. "We'll get you free." She wasn't sure if Reyna understood. She thought perhaps it was better if Reyna was unconscious. It meant she would struggle and move around less, and feel less pain.

"I'm ready," Courtney told J.G. and Jeremy over the lump in her throat. The two of them were positioned at the end of the branch, ready to give it all of their strength. Courtney had her eyes fixed on the boulder. If it moved, she would be ready to pull Reyna's arm right out of there. She knew Reyna's hand would be crushed, her fingers undoubtedly broken, but at least Reyna wouldn't be trapped anymore. And out here it was far better to have a broken hand than a broken foot or ankle. As long as they could keep walking, they would be okay.

Jeremy nodded at J.G. "I'm ready too."

Without a word, J.G. and Jeremy began to push down simultaneously on the thick tree branch. Courtney hoped the force would nudge the boulder upward, and at first, it seemed like that might happen. She saw the boulder tremble slightly, and her heart started racing faster as her fingers gripped Reyna's arm.

But then, with a crack as loud as a gunshot, the branch splintered and broke in the center. The noise made Courtney cry out in surprise. J.G. and Jeremy were both thrown off balance, and J.G. stumbled back into the snow. Jeremy stood there, looking startled, still gripping the useless branch.

"Fuck!" he swore.

J.G. was picking himself up from the snow. "Dry rot. The tree was no good. We need to find another branch and try again."

"No way." Jeremy shook his head, seemingly on the verge of a temper tantrum. "This is a dumb idea. It's not going to work."

J.G. ignored him and asked Courtney, "How's Reyna?"

"Fine," Courtney said without thinking. Then she looked down at Reyna and realized the girl was far from fine. "I mean, she's passed out again. At least I think so."

"If she's still alive, there's hope." J.G. was already looking around for another branch to use.

"Hope isn't a plan," Jeremy spat.

"It's all we have," Courtney told him.

Jeremy tossed the hatchet down in the snow. "It's useless," he said. Courtney still couldn't believe his attitude, and how he was giving up so easily. Supposedly he had a huge crush on Reyna, but he was acting like he didn't care what happened to her—or to any of them, not even himself. She never would have guessed he'd behave this way, or become so mentally fragile, but she supposed a crisis could bring out the worst in people. Still, it hadn't brought out the worst in her, or in Reyna, or even in J.G. Maybe a crisis worked like truth serum, and brought out a person's true colors, she thought.

"I think I found a good branch," J.G. called out. He'd clambered over to another tree and was testing its limbs. "Jeremy, pick up that hatchet and get over here."

Jeremy bent down and snatched up the hatchet from the snow. "Sure thing, boss," he said. "Whatever you say."

"Jeremy, just help him," Courtney implored. "Do it for Reyna."

"Okay," he relented, moving stiffly over to J.G.'s side like a zombie. "But this is never going to work . . ."

XIV

It turned out that Jeremy was right. Courtney, J.G., and Jeremy spent the entire rest of the day attempting to free Reyna. The three of them tried all kinds of permutations, but nothing worked. Even with Courtney pushing alongside J.G. and Jeremy, they hadn't been able to move the rock at all.

They also hadn't heard or seen any signs of cars behind them on the road, making Courtney certain that the road was still closed. She was amazed no police helicopters were in the sky, looking for them, or for Leonard and all the escaped convicts. Although it continued to snow sporadically, it seemed like the worst of the blizzard was over. But it was growing clear they would be stuck outside for yet another night.

Courtney was attempting to feed Reyna melted snow,

and watching the sky start to get dark, when the final moment came.

"I quit," Jeremy said, flinging down the hatchet again, like a petulant child. "It's over."

Although Courtney hated him in that moment, she also had to agree that none of their ideas had been successful. Reyna's arm was still trapped, and she was getting frailer by the moment. To make things worse, Courtney knew they had wasted an entire day of travel time, and now they were hungrier and colder than before—so hungry and cold, in fact, that the journey was starting to feel like an impossibility to her. She couldn't imagine hiking another six miles in this condition, no matter what. They were also out of Gatorade and any remaining food. Earlier, Jeremy had climbed back up the cliff and reclaimed their mostly empty backpacks, just to make sure, but there weren't even any crumbs left.

"You can't quit," Courtney said to Jeremy now, as she remained crouching over Reyna. "We need you. I need you."

"To do what?" His tone was hostile.

"If we free Reyna, we can make it out of here—"

He spoke over her: "You keep saying that, but you're deluded!" He gestured around him, waving his arms frantically like a crazy person. "Do you see any way out of here?" He pointed at Reyna's helpless body. "Is there any way out for her?" He kicked at the snow with his boot, sending up a big spray. Then he answered his own question and said, "There's no way out."

"What do you want us to do, Jeremy? Just lie down and die in the snow?"

A long silence fell, marked only by Reyna's faint moaning.

"There is a way out," J.G. finally said to Jeremy. "You just have to stop losing your cool every two seconds, and act smart enough to find it."

"Don't lecture me. I'll kick your ass again," Jeremy threatened, but there wasn't any energy behind it.

"Maybe you will, but how's that going to help anything?"

Jeremy didn't have a good comeback, so he went silent again. Reyna turned her body slightly in the snow, curling up against the rock. Courtney put her arms around her, trying to give her some warmth.

"We need each other," J.G. continued. "It's like in prison. You only survive as part of a group. Loners never make it. You have to realize you're part of a team."

"So what, you want us to become neo-Nazis like you?" Jeremy retorted. "Is that the kind of team you have in mind?"

"I'm not a neo-Nazi. In fact, I believe all people—all races—are equally fucked-up. But I do want to survive. Sometimes surviving means doing things you're not proud of. That's how life works."

"Your life, maybe. Not mine."

"Don't be too sure. You're too young to know how things will turn out for you."

"Shut up, dude. You're a loser."

"That's your opinion. But right now, it looks like life has put us on equal ground."

Courtney's mind was turning over ideas faster than she could speak. "We'll have to stay here tonight," she told J.G. and Jeremy, figuring if she talked rapidly and sounded confident, then maybe they'd listen to her. "There's no way to travel at night, and we can't leave Reyna anyway. Tomorrow morning we can try again with the boulder, when we're rested. Maybe Reyna will be more conscious, and we can get her to help us. Or maybe she'll come up with some great idea on her own."

"Maybe, maybe," Jeremy muttered, but he didn't disagree and neither did J.G.

"It's getting colder, I can feel it," J.G. added. "We'll have to light a fire tonight if we stay, despite Leonard. The fire will keep any animals away too."

Courtney didn't want to think about the animals. She knew that now she and the others were tired, hungry, and weak, natural predators would be even more of a threat. Something frightening was out there, and whether it was wolves, mountain lions, or Leonard Bell, it didn't really matter to her. Death was the thing to fear, and it could stalk them in many forms.

"So we'll light a fire and build another snow cave down here by the boulder," Courtney said, looking over at the prisoner. The sun was low on the horizon, and it was getting hard to see his features. Jeremy's face was even more shrouded in shadows from the trees. She waited for him to speak, but he didn't.

"Jer?" she asked. "What do you think of that plan?"

"Sure," he replied aimlessly.

"We better start digging, then," J.G. said. "We've got a lot of work to do."

Two hours later, they were dug in for the night. The snow cave they'd built this time wasn't as good as the other one, because they were so exhausted, and because Reyna couldn't help them. They'd tried to build the cave as a semicircle around her, by piling snow next to the boulder to protect her from the wind. It was more like a large wall with an overhang, because right on the other side of her was their fire, and it would have melted the snow if they'd made the cave stick out any further.

The fire was pathetic, Courtney thought as she crouched outside, stoking the meager flames. They hadn't been able to find enough wood or other materials to burn. The fire consisted mainly of brush and stray twigs, most of them damp. It didn't even provide a good source of light, just low flames.

The night sky was overhung with clouds, which meant the light of the moon was masked and gauzy. No stars were visible. Courtney guessed the temperature was dipping into the teens, edging closer back to the Arctic temperatures more normal for this time of year. She didn't know what they'd do if the temperature plummeted below zero. She felt colder than she'd ever been in her entire life, and she was starving and dehydrated on top of it.

Since the last of the Gatorade, they'd been drinking melted snow, but the water was so cold that it made her feel even more thirsty. Courtney was craving food so badly it felt like her stomach would implode. She was dying for something warm and filling, like pizza, and a gallon of hot chocolate. She thought of her and Reyna's favorite hangout back home—a grungy pizza joint named Sal's that never carded them—and wished they were there right now. She felt like she'd never be able to warm up again, and could only imagine the worse torture that Reyna was going through.

Fortunately, the girl had remained in a stupor, and Courtney hoped she wasn't fully aware of the pain. By now Courtney guessed that Reyna's hand was well beyond saving, even if they got it out from under the rock. At the least, she'd need some serious surgery to fix it up again.

I have to fight for us, she told herself. *Reyna's hurt, Jeremy's cracking up, and who knows what J.G. is really thinking?* Their fate depended on her actions, even the fate of Harris and Melanie, back down the road somewhere in the SUV.

J.G. and Jeremy slumped near Reyna and the fire, watching Courtney tend to it. Purplish bruises had formed on J.G.'s face from where Jeremy had struck him. Courtney noticed that neither of them were doing much to help Reyna anymore, not even J.G. with all his medical training. Perhaps he had given up on her.

"This place is hell," Jeremy said. Inexplicably, he'd

taken out his journal and had been writing something in it. It was the first time she'd ever seen hlm write openly in front of anyone. He was staring down at the pages as he spoke. Courtney couldn't help wondering if the paper might make good fuel for the fire, but she didn't suggest it. "Maybe we died in the car crash and this is hell, where we belong."

"I wish this was hell, because hell is hot," Courtney told him. "But it isn't. This is reality."

"Maybe it's both," J.G. said finally, his eyes fixed on her. "Perhaps life on earth is actually hell."

"I don't believe that." Courtney looked back at him. "When the sun comes up tomorrow—if it comes up—we're going to get that boulder off Reyna." She felt it was her responsibility now to lead the group, a role she never thought she'd be forced to take on because she wasn't as assured as Reyna. But out of necessity, she'd found an untapped reservoir of strength. She still felt uncomfortable in the role, like she was acting, or faking her way through it, but there were no other options. Still, she wished Reyna had never got injured. Courtney knew if Reyna were still okay, they'd probably already be in Pine Valley: safe, warm, and out of the snow.

"If we can't get the boulder off her tomorrow, then one of us stays and the other two go," J.G. said. "I don't want to lose another day here."

Yes, but who goes and who stays? Courtney wondered. J.G. would have to go, because only he knew the way, which meant either she or Jeremy would have to accompany him. Courtney glanced over at Jeremy, or what little of his face she could see from under the hood of his sweatshirt.

"I could stay with Reyna, and you and J.G. could find the town together," she said, although she didn't know if she could count on Jeremy and J.G. not to fight. "That would work, maybe."

"We shouldn't split up," Jeremy replied, looking up from his journal. "That's when problems happen." Courtney couldn't tell if he really thought that, or if he just didn't want to go anywhere alone with J.G. Or maybe he wanted to remain with Reyna. "We should have stayed put with Harris and Melanie. It was a big mistake to leave."

"We might have to split up again," she told him. "In case you haven't noticed, we don't have too many choices." Courtney was getting sick of these endless circular discussions about who should go and who should stay.

"I could go to town by myself," J.G. proposed. "Send help back."

"No," Jeremy said flatly. "I don't trust you. You might never send anyone for us. Why would you tell anyone we were here? It wouldn't be in your best interest. You'd disappear on us."

Although Courtney didn't think J.G. would be so heartless, the words still scared her. It was true that J.G., as an escaped convict, didn't have much to gain by going to the authorities. Was it possible he'd just abandon them?

"If I wanted to disappear, I would have done it already," J.G. pointed out. "Give me some credit."

"We'll find a solution," Courtney said, even though she wasn't sure that they would. "In the morning, we'll be rested, and the sun will be out." She was trying to stay optimistic, but Jeremy didn't seem to be listening to her, and neither did J.G.

"The fire's dying," Jeremy said in a voice of resigned exhaustion, pointing at the flickering embers. "I'll go find more wood." He put his journal away and staggered up, so tired he moved like he was drunk.

Courtney sighed and pushed herself up from Reyna. She knew it was going to be a very long night. As she maneuvered sideways through the snow, she suddenly heard J.G. hiss, "Stop!"

She ceased moving at once, puzzled and unnerved. He was crouching on his haunches, his body coiled to spring. It took her a second to realize that he'd heard something. Jeremy stopped moving too.

"What?" Courtney whispered, as quietly as she could.

J.G. cocked his head in the direction of the forest to their left. "Listen," he murmured back.

They remained silent and stationary for a long moment, until Jeremy whispered, "I don't hear anything."

Courtney didn't either, but as she continued to listen, her ears became attuned to the frequency of the forest. Underneath the lazy crackling of the dying fire, she heard all the minute noises of snow and ice shifting, and the weary creaking of tree branches. And then, beneath those sounds, she finally heard a distant, animalistic baying that was now all too familiar to her.

Jeremy heard the noises at the same moment, and their eyes locked in the darkness across the fire.

"There really is something out there," he said, forgetting to whisper, like maybe he hadn't believed it until that very moment.

"Wolves," J.G. said, in an almost thoughtful way. "It's not Leonard, it's wolves. And they know we're here."

Jeremy twitched. "How can they know that?"

"They just do." He turned back to the fire. "We need to build this up. It's the only thing that will keep us safe. They're far away now, but they're calling for each other, casting a net that's going to narrow in on us." He was looking around for potential firewood. "If they come, they'll go after Reyna first. She's the weakest."

In the fading firelight, Jeremy's face was caught between fear and disbelief. Courtney guessed that his expression probably mirrored hers. Wolves, she was thinking to herself. *As if we haven't been through enough.*

"Maybe they won't find us," she said to J.G.

"Maybe, but I learned a long time ago to expect the worst. If there are wolves and humans in an isolated environment for long enough, eventually they'll meet. But if we get the fire built up, and take turns keeping watch, perhaps we'll be okay . . ." He peered back out into the darkness. "Unless the wolves are really hungry."

Courtney heard the baying sounds in the distance again. Maybe it was her imagination playing tricks on her, but the noises already sounded a little closer. As her stomach clenched up, she realized the baying sounds now seemed to be coming from slightly different directions, as though the source had multiplied. She didn't want to think about the implications of that.

"The fire," J.G. said urgently, apparently noticing the same thing. "Get to it."

The three of them started digging in frantic haste, desperately trying to unearth any wood from the depths of the snow. Most of the wood was wet and useless, Courtney knew, but they could split or break some of the lumber and get to the dry sections inside. She remembered Reyna telling her right after the crash that people burned the money from their wallets to stay warm. If Courtney had any paper money, or a wallet, at that moment she would have happily tossed all of it into the fire. She wished she had more clothes on so she could take off another layer and burn it as fuel. Anything to get the fire larger and keep the wolves away from them.

J.G. knelt by the fire, using his chained hands to haul wood across it. Jeremy was swinging the hatchet and trying to cut down branches. Courtney came over to the fire at J.G.'s side, and attempted to get sparks to catch by blowing on them. The fire was still struggling, but there was a degree of improvement. Courtney just didn't know if it would be enough.

She suddenly heard a faint voice calling for her and realized it was Reyna. She immediately rushed over to her friend and bent her head down next to her.

"I'm so . . . cold," Reyna was saying. She was shivering badly enough that it was hard for her to talk. "I don't feel good. I need to get warm."

Courtney had never heard Reyna sound so sick before. She clutched Reyna's good hand and squeezed it. "We're making the fire bigger, as big as we can." She didn't mention anything about the wolves. "You're going to warm up soon." She squeezed Reyna's hand again. There was no response. When she glanced down, Reyna looked like she'd fallen back into her comatose state. Courtney didn't know if it was shock, or hypothermia, or both. She turned back to the fire.

Eventually, the fire was as large as they could make it. They had exhausted all the usable wood from the surrounding area. The wood that was too damp, or too green, just sputtered, refusing to light. Because the fire was larger, it cast more light and made more noise. Still, every now and then, the sounds of the wolves were audible above it. Courtney couldn't tell if the animals were still getting closer or not.

J.G. took the first watch, so Courtney huddled up next to Reyna, sharing warmth with her as she watched the flames. Jeremy was on the other side of Reyna, so the injured girl was partially sandwiched between them. Courtney hoped their body heat would help keep her alive.

At first, Courtney was positive she wouldn't be able to fall asleep, because she was so scared and cold. Yet she was also pushed to her limits mentally and physically. This debacle has to end sometime, she told herself, imagining how amazingly great it would feel when they got rescued. *We can't be stuck forever.*

Courtney continued watching the fire through the narrow opening left for her eyes between her hat and her scarf. Its yellow flames were oddly soothing, a palliative against her fear. And at some point, she drifted into sleep.

Courtney began dreaming of a vacation she'd taken with her parents to San Diego once, a long time ago when she was a little girl. In the dream, it was all sun, palm trees, and sweltering heat. She could feel drops of sweat trickling down the back of her neck as she walked down the street, her flip-flops smacking the pavement. But something was all wrong, and she realized she couldn't find her parents anywhere.

She started to cry in the dream, and it woke her up. She suddenly remembered where she was, and felt the freezing tears streaking her cheeks. She wiped them away roughly and closed her eyes again. She refused to allow herself to think about her parents.

Soon Courtney drifted sideways into a different kind of dream, one much closer to reality, in which she was being pursued by some nameless, faceless entity. It was dark and amorphous, tracking her as she tried to run through the snow. She didn't know what it was, only that it wanted to do her harm. She wasn't even sure whether it was some sort of monster, or if it was a person.

Not long afterward, she woke up again with a start to the sound of Jeremy screaming—and her entire world crashing down around her.

XV

The fire had died down at some point during the night, and its remaining glow cast barely enough light for Courtney to see. Only a few branches were still burning, while most looked like mere embers. Courtney was shaking with cold because water and snow had seeped into her clothes. Screaming sounds rang in her ears as she tried to move her frozen limbs.

Jeremy was to her left, yelling in terror as he waved the hatchet around. Courtney couldn't see his assailant, but she knew at once what was happening. All around her she heard the barking and yipping sounds of the wolf pack, darting in and out of the trees, racing across the snow. They skittered on top of it with their claws, almost as though they were skating.

J.G. was crouched on the other side of the fire, right

next to it. He was trying to pull one of the lone burning branches out to use as a weapon.

"Help me!" Jeremy screamed at Courtney, over the sounds of the wolves, as she tried to process what was going on. "They're everywhere!"

Courtney was too terrified to speak. She caught her first full glimpse of a wolf, darting over a ridge. It was gray and sinewy, the size of a dog, but far more vicious-looking. Its shimmering gold eyes caught the remnants of the firelight for an instant and reflected it back at her. As it turned away, she noticed that its mouth was open, and saw a glimpse of sharp fangs. She didn't know how many wolves were out there in the forest, but it seemed like a lot.

How many wolves are in a wolf pack? she wondered, the words sounding like a children's riddle. She realized she should have asked J.G., but now it was too late.

Courtney didn't realize that she was standing there paralyzed by fear until she felt something collide with her. She gasped in surprise and spun around, afraid it was one of the wolves, but it was J.G. He'd managed to get the burning branch out of the fire and was holding it awkwardly in his shackled hands like a torch.

"Take this to Reyna!" he hissed. "Protect her."

She didn't argue with him. Courtney grabbed the branch and held it out in front of her. Even though it wasn't much of a weapon, she thought she could use the light to keep the wolves away. And if that didn't work, maybe she could use it as a bludgeon.

As Jeremy continued to scream and lunge at the darkness with his hatchet, Courtney crouched at Reyna's side. She was afraid a wolf might have got there already, but Reyna was okay. Courtney knelt over her friend, swinging the burning branch out in front of them for protection. Reyna seemed to be unconscious, or in a deep sleep nearing hibernation.

"Rey!" she yelled. "Wake up!" As she stared back into the forest, looking for the wolves, she heard Reyna stir and murmur something. Without looking back down, she said, "The wolves found us!" Reyna mumbled vague words in return, but it was clear to Courtney that she wasn't going to wake up all the way.

Courtney heard a sudden crash and saw another wolf bounding through the trees beyond the fire. Its body was wraithlike, as though it had been conjured up from the snow itself. As it disappeared from view behind a snow-bank, Courtney heard a high-pitched baying sound come from the opposite direction, above the cliff that Reyna had fallen down. She turned to look, pointing the torch up in its direction, but there was nothing there.

The wolves are circling us, she suddenly thought, frightened by their intelligence. *I have to keep them away.* Courtney hoped the attack would stop soon, if the wolves couldn't easily get what they wanted, but she wasn't certain. Perhaps the attack would continue until morning. If that were the case, then it might just be a war of attrition, and Courtney guessed the wolves could win that one. We're the interlopers here, she thought, not them. She knew that to these wolves, human beings were nothing more than a potential meal.

As she guarded Reyna, Courtney watched J.G. drag another burning log from the fire. Jeremy seemed to be lost in his own world, ranting and slicing at thin air. He wasn't helping J.G., nor had he figured out that J.G.'s strategy was probably worth emulating. He was just howling incoherently, like the wolves themselves. Fortunately, he remained close enough to the fire that the wolves weren't coming near him, at least not yet.

Courtney watched in horror as two more wolves burst from the trees ahead of them, about twenty feet away, one after the other, each one yipping and growling. They ran forward, and only slowed their pace when J.G. swung his makeshift torch back and forth.

"Git!" he yelled at them savagely, drawing yellow streaks in the darkness with the burning branch. "Go on! Git!"

The first wolf slunk low to the snow, its paws splayed out on either side for balance. It took another tentative step forward, as though preparing to spring at him. J.G. jabbed the torch in its direction with a yell and got it to back off. It disappeared into the darkness, but its companion remained, lurking and watching carefully from a safer distance.

At that instant, Courtney was distracted by a soft scrabbling sound above her on the boulder. She turned and swung the torch upward, her heart in her throat. What she saw made her scream in raw terror. Perched above her and Reyna on top of the icy rock was one of the wolves. Somehow it had sneaked up there without them hearing it. Its yellow eyes were fixed directly on her, and its haunches were raised and quivering in preparation for an assault.

The wolf growled, showing teeth. Courtney had no doubt it was about to spring on her and Reyna. She knew the only thing that prevented them from getting mauled was the piece of burning wood in her hands. Even though the branch was heavy, fear gave her new strength, and she whipped it upward, trying to scare the wolf away.

The wolf dodged the blow, moving sideways with unbelievable grace, its paws negotiating the icy surface with ease. It took a half step back from the edge of the rock and bared its fangs again. It was looking down at something past Courtney, with ravenous glee, and it took her a moment to understand it was eyeing Reyna's body.

"No!" Courtney yelled at the wolf. "Go away!" She didn't know if it would have any effect to yell like that, but it had worked when J.G. did it. She waved the torch around, hoping to make the wolf back up even further.

The wolf continued to look down at her and Reyna, sniffing the air with its snout. By the light of the flames, Courtney could see that its fangs were blackened with decay, although the tips looked as finely honed as steak knives.

Courtney heard J.G. yell something at her, but she

couldn't pay him any mind because she'd locked eyes with the wolf again. Even though she was aware the fire was keeping it away, she felt somehow that it was also the force of her own stare. She feared that if she looked away for a second, the wolf would leap on them, and other wolves would follow.

The wolf never blinked as it kept staring at her. Its eyes were tiny circles of bright light, but they looked dead inside, like shark's eyes. Courtney kept trying to wave the torch in front of its face, even though her arms were throbbing. She knew if another wolf came up behind her, she wouldn't be able to keep both away at once. She didn't know how smart wolves were, but she guessed if they were hungry enough they could be pretty resourceful.

"Leave us alone!" she yelled at the wolf again, but it remained fixed in place, still watching. "You can't have us!"

Suddenly, from her left, a burning object flew through the air and smashed into the top of the boulder. Embers sparked across its surface, showering the wolf in a cascade of fire. Within a millisecond, the wolf was gone, tumbling off the other side with a startled yelp. Courtney didn't understand what had happened until she saw J.G. standing there. He had taken his torch and hurled it at the wolf on the rock. He was saying something to Courtney now, but she was so frazzled it was hard to focus on his words.

"What?" she called back to him. As she did so, she

noticed that an eerie silence was falling. The yelping, and the patter of wolves' feet on snow, was fading. Courtney could barely believe it, but it seemed as though the wolves were retreating. She stood there listening as their sounds disappeared into the distance.

"It's over," J.G. said to Courtney, as he slowly approached. "For now."

"Holy shit, that was scary," she managed to say back to him.

Jeremy was still stabbing the air with the hatchet, like a punch-drunk prizefighter. Courtney realized he'd done nothing to help her, J.G., or Reyna. He hadn't even really helped himself, she thought. He'd just got lucky.

"They're really gone," J.G. said to Courtney as he reached the rock and leaned against it. "Yours was the last one." His voice was thick and weary, and Courtney could hear the relief in it. "We're safe, at least for a while. Maybe the rest of the night."

"How do you know?" Her words were as shaky as her hands. "You're just guessing, aren't you? You don't really know anything, not for sure—it's all just assumptions."

"We scared them. We weren't easy prey." He took in a deep breath and then pushed it out again. Courtney saw that blood was dripping down from where the cuffs had gouged into his flesh again. "We were too much work."

Courtney tried to assimilate this news. She felt like her thoughts were muddy. "What if they come back?"

"Then we'll have another fight on our hands."

Courtney heard Jeremy raving even louder, so she looked over at him.

"Fuckers!" he was screaming. He still hadn't noticed that the wolves had dispersed.

We're going to make it, Courtney recited over and over in her head, trying to hypnotize herself into believing it. She knew there would be no more sleep that night, no matter what. Maybe no sleep for a long time. From here on out, it would be a grueling vigil, waiting to see if the wolves would return.

"We have to build up that fire again," J.G. said. His eyes were roaming around as he talked to her, as though he were still on the lookout.

"Build it up with what?" Courtney replied hopelessly. The branch she was holding was still burning at its tip, but just barely.

"With anything we can scrounge." J.G.'s eyes found hers. "The bigger we make the fire, the better our chances. You still want to live, don't you?" She nodded, and he coughed and spat onto the snow. "I didn't make it through all those years in prison just to become some wolf's dinner. My life is worth more than that." Courtney didn't disagree. "So is yours."

Jeremy stumbled toward the two of them. He had stopped yelling, but he was gripping the hatchet tightly, ready to lunge at anything that moved.

"The wolves are gone, Jer," Courtney told him.

He didn't speak, he just looked blank.

"We scared them away," she continued. "We won."

She could tell she still wasn't getting through to him. "We're alone out here now . . ."

"The fire," J.G. prodded. "Get to it, Jeremy."

Like an automaton, Jeremy shuffled slowly toward the dying flames with the hatchet in hand.

"Morning will be here soon," J.G. said, as the two of them followed after Jeremy. "I'll be glad to see that sunrise." Courtney could tell he'd said the words just to cheer her up. She knew morning was many hours away.

Only then did something occur to her, that J.G. had risked his own life when he'd thrown the burning tree branch at the wolf.

"You saved me," she told him gravely, feeling oddly sheepish that she hadn't thanked him already. "Thank you for doing that, I mean, with the torch."

He nodded, but said, "Thank me when we're out of here."

"I will," Courtney promised him. "And we *will* get out of here." Despite her fear, she was determined not to become a victim to the wolves, or any other terrors the wilderness might offer. She started digging around in the snow, trying to find more wood. She peered back at Reyna, a few paces away, to make sure she was okay. Reyna wasn't looking so good. Her lips were so cracked and chewed up that even more blood had run onto her chin and frozen there.

You might make it, but will she? a voice in Courtney's head asked. She pushed the voice away, trying to submerge it with positive energy. Reyna has to make it, she told herself, because she couldn't imagine life without her best friend. She remembered the first time she'd met Reyna, all those years ago, in a junior high social studies class. Their teacher had been a boring drone, and they'd spent their time passing notes back and forth. The two of them had clicked right away, bonding over their shared taste in music, books, and movies. She was as close to Reyna as to her own family, if not closer.

With luck and dedication, Courtney and J.G. managed to keep the fire alive for the next several hours, until the sky finally began to grow lighter. It moved from black, to dark gray, and then to a strange gray-green color. The sky was still covered with thick clouds that blocked the sun's rays, yet any degree of light was a huge improvement over the night before. Courtney was also relieved that it hadn't started snowing again.

There had been no sleep for any of them except Reyna. It had been a long night, during which every stray sound made Courtney leap up in alarm, but the wolves had not returned. In the morning light, faint traces of their paw prints were visible in the top crust of snow. Even these lingering remnants of their presence spooked Courtney. She didn't think she would be able to spend another night outside and still keep a grip on her sanity.

After she checked on Reyna, Courtney glanced over at Jeremy. He was walking around in a daze by the fire, swinging his arms around and trying to keep warm. He'd fallen very quiet and Courtney wondered what he was thinking.

"You okay?" she asked him.

He nodded. "I have to—" he began, like he was talking to himself, but then he stopped.

She sensed that maybe he wanted to tell her something, so she gently prodded him. "Yeah? What is it?"

"I—" he haltingly began again. "I have a confession. I need to tell you what I've done."

Courtney was confused. "What are you talking about?" She wondered if it was about how he hadn't helped during the wolf attack.

"There're some things you don't know," he continued. "I'm too ashamed to say . . ."

"It's okay, Jer," she told him in a placating tone of voice. "We're all trying to do our best here. Don't worry. Just tell me."

"I'm afraid you'll think I'm a bad person."

"No, I won't. But what do you mean?"

She wanted to bring him out of his shell, and thought she was making progress, but he suddenly rubbed his forehead like he'd reconsidered, and the moment passed. "Never mind," he muttered. "Doesn't matter."

He turned his back and walked away before she could ask him any other questions. It was extremely weird, but Courtney didn't have the energy to follow up on it. She stared after him, wondering what his deal was.

J.G. was also on his feet, at the margin of the clearing, pissing into the snow at the base of a tree. She could tell by his posture that he was exhausted too. He was so thin, and he was wearing the least clothes of any of them. She wondered how he managed to keep from collapsing. Perhaps it was adrenaline that was getting him through, or maybe he'd built up a tolerance in prison to harsh situations.

She looked away, into the heart of the fire. They would have to come up with some kind of plan, or else they were all going to die. She thought about Harris and Melanie waiting for them back at the SUV. It had been a while since the two of them were in her thoughts. Were they even still alive? Had Melanie bled to death? She felt bad for them, because she knew they had no idea what was happening. They probably expected a helicopter or a snowmobile to come in and rescue them already, but that clearly wasn't going to happen soon.

This whole trip has been nothing but bad luck, Courtney thought. One tragedy after another. If only they'd crashed closer to Pine Valley, instead of in such a remote location, everything would have been fine. Or if they'd just stuck to the main road instead of trying a shortcut. But it was too late to turn back the clock now. Courtney knew they'd have to work with what little they had.

Intrusive thoughts flooded her brain, distracting her. Despite the vow not to think about her parents, she kept worrying about them, how they'd feel if they lost another child. My parents might never see me again, she thought. *Or if they do, it might be my body, and I won't be in it anymore.* She didn't know what happened when a person died—whether there was a heaven or a hell, or what—but she definitely didn't want to find out.

She had stupid thoughts too, embarrassing ones. *If I die out here, then I'll still be a virgin,* she thought numbly. *I'll die without ever having sex.* It didn't seem like it should matter, but it did. She wished that she and Chris had never broken up. It would be sad to die without a boyfriend.

A thin, scratchy voice broke her reverie: "Courtney," she heard the voice say. She realized it was Reyna, and went over at once to the girl's side. Reyna's face was mottled with bruises, almost as badly as J.G.'s was, but her dark eyes looked brighter for the first time since she'd got trapped by the boulder.

"We're okay. The wolves are gone, and we're safe," Courtney heard herself babble in a falsely cheerful voice. *Safe: what a joke.*

"Wolves?" Reyna looked confused.

"They came in the night for us. A whole pack of them. We used the fire to keep them away. J.G. saved us."

"Jesus."

That word, that name, was sounding so inadequate it could never embody all the shock and horror of the situation, no matter how many times it got invoked.

Courtney saw panic in Reyna's eyes. She didn't want to scare her, so she said, "The important thing is that we're okay, and it's morning. The wolves won't come back while it's light. J.G. said so."

Reyna looked like she didn't really believe that but was willing to play along. "I can't feel my arm," she said. "Nothing below my elbow. It's all gone." Courtney didn't know what to say. "I used to be able to feel my wrist, but now there's not even any pain down there." Reyna grimaced. "I'm guessing that's not a good sign."

"Listen, we're going to get that boulder off you. J.G. and I are working on a new plan." This was, of course, a lie, but Courtney couldn't help it. She just wanted to keep Reyna's spirits up and give her hope.

Reyna looked abruptly stricken. "I feel dizzy. I have to sit up." She tried to get vertical, propping herself up against the rock, her face contorted in agony. "My bicep is cramping!" Courtney helped her, making sure Reyna didn't hurt herself by twisting her arm too much. When Reyna was sitting, and the muscle spasm had passed, she looked Courtney dead in the eyes. "Did you know that I have a plan too?" she said, sounding a little woozy. "I saw it in my dreams last night. I've been having such crazy dreams. . . ."

Courtney swallowed hard. "Crazier than our reality?" Out of the corner of her eye she could see Jeremy puttering around with the hatchet again while J.G. built up the fire.

"I know what we have to do now," Reyna continued. Her gaze became unflinching. "We still got that hatchet?"

Courtney nodded, hoping Reyna wasn't going where Courtney thought she was. "Jeremy has it."

Reyna smiled grimly. "Then we need to put it to use." She glanced down at her trapped arm, as her meaning became fully apparent. "On me."

XVI

"No way," Courtney said, stunned, as Reyna's words trailed away. "Are you insane? There has to be another answer."

"Is there?" Reyna asked softly. "I'd rather lose my hand than my life. Wouldn't you? Wouldn't anyone?"

"No." Courtney felt like she was going to throw up. "Who's going to cut it off for you? Not me, that's for sure. I bet Jeremy won't either. No one's going to help you mutilate yourself." She struggled to suppress her mounting hysteria at Reyna's suggestion. "We just need to try moving the boulder again."

"We tried that. It didn't work." Reyna's words had become clipped and precise, as though she were confident this was the only solution.

"Well, let's keep trying!"

"My hand is fucked-up, Courtney. It's dead already." She paused. "I'm not scared anymore. I'm not desperate. I'm just being pragmatic."

Courtney shook her head. "You're out of luck. I refuse to do it, and Jeremy's a nervous wreck, and J.G. has handcuffs on. There's no way I'm going to let you hurt yourself. I can stay here with you while Jeremy and J.G. walk to town and they'll send someone—"

"It's not your decision," Reyna interrupted. "We'll be dead by then, either from exposure or from the wolves. I want to live."

"Me too! That's what I've been trying to do. Keep us alive." Courtney was getting frustrated. "If we cut your hand off, you'll bleed to death."

Reyna had clearly thought this out already, because when she spoke, she sounded quite lucid. "No, I won't. The blood vessels are already constricted from the pressure of the rock, and from the cold. If we tie a tourniquet around my arm before we do it, I'll be fine. Besides, J.G.'s a medic."

Courtney couldn't believe they were discussing something so horrific and brutal as amputation in such logical terms. She knew if she were in Reyna's position, she would be screaming, cursing, and crying. She certainly wouldn't be suggesting that they hack off her hand. In fact, her own hands and wrists were starting to ache with sympathy pains, so she jammed them in her pockets.

"This kind of thing has been done before," Reyna continued, seemingly oblivious to Courtney's horror. "I saw a documentary about it. A climber in Utah got trapped in a ravine, all alone with no food or water. He was out there for days until he finally cut his arm off with a pocket knife. It took him six hours, because he had to get through the bones."

Courtney turned away, revolted.

"It was the only way for him to survive," Reyna explained with preternatural calm. "He made it out of the ravine and hiked back to his car. Then he drove himself to the hospital."

"But it's your *hand*. How are you going to do anything with one hand? This isn't some story, or some textbook case. This is you."

"It won't change anything. I can still be a doctor with one hand. But I can't be a doctor if I'm dead."

"There's got to be another way."

"I hope there is, but if there isn't . . . it's okay." She reached out and grabbed at the sleeve of Courtney's jacket. "I'm not scared, Court. My hand is dead, but the rest of me isn't."

Maybe Reyna hit her head in the fall, Courtney thought, because no sane person would advocate this kind of thing. She was prepared to argue more with Reyna when the girl coughed, and Courtney saw some blood come out. She thought for a moment it was just from Reyna's torn lips, but then even more blood came, and she realized that the blood was coming from inside her friend.

Courtney knelt down and said, "You're bleeding, Rey. You're hurt."

Reyna smiled. "Tell me something I don't know." She wiped the blood away with her good hand and looked at it on her sleeve.

J.G. appeared behind Courtney, leaning over her shoulder to gaze at Reyna. He saw the blood but didn't comment on it. Courtney wondered if the blood meant that Reyna had internal injuries, or if she was getting pneumonia or something. But like Reyna said, J.G. was a medic, Courtney reminded herself. If there were some way for him to help, he probably would have thought of it already.

"You'll do it, won't you?" Reyna suddenly asked the prisoner as he watched her.

"Do what?"

Courtney knew he didn't understand, so she said, "Reyna wants you to amputate her hand."

J.G.'s expression didn't change at all. No shadows moved behind his eyes.

"I've been telling her we'll find another way to free her," Courtney interjected, "but she's not listening. There has to be a way, right?"

Reyna looked past her, directly at J.G. "Will you do it?" she asked, her voice firmer, louder. It almost sounded like a challenge, or a dare.

J.G. stared back at her. Finally he said, "One condition."

"What?"

"That your friends get these cuffs off me. I can't do it with them on."

"Why not?"

He looked annoyed, as though he thought Reyna was being stupid. "I can't work with my hands chained because it's a precise operation. I have to get the right angles. I might need to tie off a vein. I could screw up and get things wrong . . . You don't want that."

Courtney felt herself being reduced to the role of a horrified onlooker. She stood up abruptly and said, "This is crazy!" She saw Jeremy over by the fire with the hatchet, so she yelled out, "Jer! Get over here!"

Despite his recent descent into general lunacy, she was hoping that maybe this fresh trauma would snap him back to his senses. And given his crush on Reyna, assuming it still existed, surely he wouldn't want to see her hand get mangled.

Jeremy turned in their direction and stumbled over as Courtney, Reyna, and J.G. all watched him. There was some stubble on his face, and his hair was disheveled.

"Yeah?" he asked when he got there, twirling the hatchet lazily like a baton. His eyes were bleary and streaked with tiny red veins, as though he had a hangover. There was a dullness to them, Courtney noticed, suggesting some part of his spirit had been broken. Since his earlier attempt to talk to her, he had seemingly regressed even more.

"Reyna wants to—" Courtney began again, but Reyna stopped her.

"Let me tell it. It's my choice."

Courtney fell silent, out of despair.

"Jeremy, I'm going to ask you to do something for me." Reyna looked up at him. He was a dark silhouette against the cloudy gray sky. "I need you to use that hatchet to get the handcuffs off J.G., okay?"

"Huh?" Jeremy asked, the noise sounding like a groan.

Reyna repeated herself, and then added, "It's okay. J.G. isn't going to hurt us. He's going to help me get free so we can find the town, all right?" Courtney noticed she was speaking gently and slowly, like she would to a child. Obviously she understood that something wasn't right with Jeremy anymore, that he was undergoing a breakdown. "After last night, I think it's clear J.G. is on our side. He's one of us."

Jeremy looked over at Courtney as if seeking reassurance. But that was the last thing she wanted to give him. "Reyna wants J.G. to cut off her fucking hand, get it?" Courtney said bluntly, hoping to shock Jeremy out of his stupor. "That's why she wants you to break the handcuffs."

Jeremy didn't even blink. Instead he said, "I'm cold."

Courtney felt like giving up. She didn't know who else to turn to. The little voice in the back of her mind piped up again.

Maybe if this is what everyone wants, then it really is for the best, the voice said. *We'd get out of here faster. We could leave today, right now, in fact. We could be home by tomorrow. Reyna's right—her hand is already gone. We'd be doing her a big favor.*

"See that rock?" J.G. said to Jeremy. He was pointing

at a small granite boulder sticking out of the snow at the bottom of the cliff next to them. "If I stretch my arms apart and get the chain taut, enough blows from the hatchet will break it."

Jeremy looked at the small boulder. His eyes were empty and guileless.

"Will you do it?" Reyna asked him. "Do it for me?" Now there was something oddly seductive about her tone. "I'd be really grateful . . ."

Jeremy slowly nodded.

Courtney sank to the snow and crouched there. "We shouldn't do this," she murmured. "It's wrong. It's too hasty. We can think of another way." No one was listening to her anymore.

J.G. was over at the rock, kneeling and trying to position himself. He stretched the chain across the icy, gray surface, its silver links glistening. Jeremy lumbered over with the hatchet, standing above him.

"You're doing good," Reyna called out to him weakly.

J.G. tilted his head back. Courtney thought that he looked a little nervous. "Just don't hit me by accident when you swing," he told Jeremy.

Jeremy nodded again, like he'd lost the power of speech.

Courtney didn't know how strong the cuffs were, but she guessed Jeremy and the hatchet were powerful enough to break the chain if they hit it hard enough.

She looked at Reyna and said one last time, "Are you sure this is what you want?"

There was no doubt on Reyna's face. In fact, she wore a look of acceptance and serenity. "I want my freedom."

"Ready when you are," J.G. told Jeremy. Then he arched his head and neck backward and straightened his arms as far as they could go. Jeremy raised the hatchet. With dismay, Courtney saw that his hands were shaking. J.G. saw it too, and looked even more nervous, but he didn't tell Jeremy to stop.

The first blow was way too weak, and the hatchet blade glanced off the chain links without even leaving a dent. Then came a second blow, and a third, followed by a fourth. With each concussive repetition, it seemed like Jeremy hit the chain and the rock harder, so hard that sparks flew off it. The blade was coming down within inches from J.G.'s hands, but he never flinched, and he kept his eyes open the whole time.

Courtney lost track of the blows, but finally, after about twenty of them, there was a cracking sound, and the chain suddenly elongated and snapped in two. J.G. fell back in the snow, a free man. He stretched his arms out on either side of him like he was preparing to make snow angels. Jeremy stood there, out of breath, holding the hatchet.

Courtney realized she'd been holding her breath, so she let out a long, white lungful of smoke into the frigid air.

J.G. got to his feet and brushed the snow off himself. "See? Easy."

Now that his hands were free, he could finally dress

himself normally. Shaking in the cold, he managed to put some top layers of clothes back on, pulling the sleeves of a jacket over the broken handcuffs. The remnants of the chain hung down from both cuffs like stray silver threads.

"Give me the hatchet," he instructed Jeremy. Jeremy obeyed automatically, in some kind of semi-somnambulant state. Courtney was surprised, because she thought he'd resist giving the weapon to the prisoner, but he didn't.

Next, J.G. walked over to Reyna.

Courtney decided to make one final attempt to delay the amputation. "Reyna's not going to be able to walk anywhere with her hand cut off," she said to J.G., the words coming out breathy instead of strong like she intended. She cleared her throat and tried again. "She'll be in too much pain. We'll end up stuck here for good. Think about it. We can't afford to fuck this up."

J.G. swiveled his head to look at her. Courtney saw the same stubborn look in his gray-blue eyes as she saw in Reyna's dark ones. They had the same strength of will.

In that moment, she felt sorry for both of them, and also slightly afraid of both of them. She realized there was nothing she could do to prevent J.G. from cutting off Reyna's hand: the train had already left the station.

"Make it quick," Reyna said to J.G.

"Promise." He knelt down to inspect her trapped arm. Then he took hold of it gently, pushing her sleeve back and moving his liberated fingers up and down in a gesture close to a caress. "I'm going to make a lateral separation across your radius and ulna, right above your wrist," he said. "This hatchet isn't sharp anymore, but I still think I can do it with one good strike. It might take two, though. Or three."

"That's fine," Reyna said.

J.G. dug in the snow for a while and came up with a short piece of wood. He wiped it off on his pant leg. "When you're ready, put this in your mouth and bite down on it. This procedure is going to hurt."

"My whole arm is numb."

"Then you're lucky." He handed her the wood, and Reyna fingered it with her good hand. Then J.G. picked up one of the shirts they'd layered on top of Reyna and tore off a long piece of fabric. Courtney recognized the shirt—it was one of Jeremy's. J.G. wrapped the fabric around Reyna's arm, just below the elbow, and created a makeshift tourniquet.

Courtney stood in dismay, watching the scene unfold. Jeremy was off to her left, muttering to himself again, lost in a reverie.

"Now, just to confirm, you want me to do this, right?" J.G. asked Reyna. "I don't want to get accused of a crime later on. I'm doing this because you need me to, because you asked me to."

Reyna slipped the piece of wood between her teeth. "Yes. Hurry up." The words were somewhat muffled, but they were still decipherable.

J.G. looked at Courtney. "You'll be my witness. You can see I'm trying to help her, not hurt her. In case there's any dispute when we get to Pine Valley." He stepped back abruptly and walked over to the fire. "I have to sterilize the implement," he said, as he held the hatchet's blade over the low flames. "The heat will also help cauterize the wound."

Reyna was already biting down on the piece of wood in preparation. Courtney felt an unbelievable sadness and fatigue. She knelt down and stroked Reyna's hair. Now that it was decided, the only thing she could do was be supportive.

"I'm here for you," was all she said.

J.G. walked back over with the hatchet and stood over his willing victim, as Courtney stepped aside. "Reyna, it's time," he said, swinging the hatchet back over his shoulder, like some medieval warrior.

"Good," was Reyna's barely audible reply. "Do it before I puss out and change my mind . . ."

Courtney shut her eyes. She didn't want to watch. At the last second, she realized she should have plugged her fingers in her ears too, but it was too late. She heard the dull, wet thud of the first blow as metal intersected with flesh.

The wood must have fallen out of Reyna's mouth, because Reyna started screaming. There were no words, it was just an incoherent howl of agony verging on madness.

Courtney opened her eyes, despite herself. Jeremy

had fallen to one knee in the snow and was trying to throw up.

"Fuck," J.G. said. Courtney didn't hear it, because of Reyna's screams, but she saw him mouth the word. She looked down and saw that the first blow hadn't got the job done, not even partway. There was splintered bone sticking out from a mass of muscles and bloody meat. It looked fake, like some gruesome, tasteless Halloween decoration. Bright red blood was sluicing down into the snow.

J.G. raised the hatchet and swung again with savage force. This time the blade cleaved through the remaining flesh, and Reyna rolled away from the boulder, her screams evolving into sobs.

Courtney raced over to help her. Blood was steadily pulsing from severed arteries. J.G. was at Reyna's side too, tightening the tourniquet. He'd tossed the hatchet back down in the snow. "You're going to be okay," J.G. said. "It went well." He sounded sincere and confident, like a trauma surgeon consulting with a patient's terrified family. "The bleeding will stop. Take deep, slow breaths." Reyna continued crying. She was trying to clutch her stump, but it was too painful, so she kept rolling around in the snow, turning the white into red.

Courtney stumbled back to give J.G. room. "You're doing great, Reyna," she said, her words sounding ridiculous. But she wanted to say something to let Reyna know she was right there, pulling for her. She was crying too, but she was trying to hide it because she didn't want to scare Reyna.

Courtney tried to focus on the positive, what little of it there was. At least Reyna is free now, Courtney told herself. *And that means all of us are free.* Free to keep walking and get to the safety of town, where they could find a doctor. Of course, Reyna would first have to survive her brutal surgery, and not go into shock or succumb to blood loss. Courtney hoped J.G. had some tricks up his sleeve to prevent either of those things from happening.

"How's she doing?" she asked J.G. nervously. Reyna had fallen mostly silent, except for occasional muffled cries. J.G. was straddling her, trying to get the bleeding to stop. He had stanched its flow somewhat and was adding another T-shirt tourniquet to her arm.

"She'll live," he told Courtney tersely, sounding preoccupied with his work.

Thank God, Courtney thought. But J.G. couldn't know for sure. He wasn't God. He couldn't predict what might happen to Reyna if they didn't get help soon.

Courtney looked up at the dark sky above them and wondered if God even existed in a place like this, where such terrible things were made to happen. Please exist, she prayed urgently to whatever unknowable presence might be out there. *Give us a sign. Give us some help. Give us anything . . .*

As expected, she received no immediate response.

XVII

Courtney, J.G., Jeremy, and Reyna spent the remainder of the morning resting by the campsite. Reyna made as much of a recovery as could be expected. She was weak and pale, but she was talking again, and relieved to be free from the prison of the boulder. Somehow she had avoided going into shock so far. She didn't mention the bloody, swaddled stump that now existed in place of her left hand. Courtney kept trying not to stare at it, but it was hard to keep her eyes away.

J.G. had used a combination of ice wraps and tourniquets to stop the bleeding. Now there were torn-up clothes wrapped around the end of the stump, forming a strange, lumpy bulge.

"How do you feel?" Courtney asked Reyna at one point, feeling nervous and not knowing what to say. All her words seemed forced. *What do you say to someone who just got their hand amputated?* There was no Hallmark card for that one.

"It doesn't hurt too much," Reyna answered. "It's just numb like before." But her voice was even thinner, and she looked exhausted and very frail sitting there in the snow, clutching her damaged arm. Courtney knew she was lying about the pain.

J.G. continued to check on Reyna and monitor her wound. Courtney and J.G. were taking turns melting snow and giving it to Reyna to drink. J.G. had told them if they could keep Reyna hydrated, then she would be able to recover somewhat and not succumb to shock. However, he'd also said that in the long run, no amount of melted snow could ever make up for all the blood loss.

Courtney imagined that if it had been her own arm that got amputated, she would have gone straight into shock and died, just from the horror of it. She guessed that compared to Reyna, she was a bit of a wimp— afraid of pain, afraid of confrontation, and afraid of death. Courtney knew that Reyna's life would never be the same, that Reyna had lost something she could never regain, no matter what. But Courtney guessed that Reyna wasn't allowing herself to dwell on those thoughts right now.

In some ways, Jeremy was struggling more than Reyna was. He'd climbed back up to the top of the cliff, picking and clawing his way up rocks, ice, and snow, and was sitting there, lost in thought. He had reclaimed the hatchet at some point and was holding it across his lap, stroking it idly as though it were a living thing. Courtney noticed that he could barely bring himself to look in Reyna's direction. He hadn't said more than a couple words to her since the improvised surgery. Courtney felt let down by him and angry on Reyna's behalf too. When they'd needed him the most, he'd allowed himself to mentally collapse and go into a catatonic shell.

I want to collapse too, Courtney thought. But she knew that she couldn't let herself do that.

"We're going to have to start walking again," J.G. said, standing by the fire. "Soon."

"I thought we were going to let Reyna rest some more," Courtney replied.

J.G. gestured at the sky. "Still not snowing. We can cover all nine and a half klicks to Pine Valley in the daylight, maybe—"

Courtney stopped him. "Klicks?"

"A klick is one kilometer," he explained. Courtney realized J.G. had lapsed back into military-speak. Perhaps their current predicament reminded him of a war zone. "Nine and a half klicks is six miles. The more ground we cover now, the better. If we wait, infection will set in and she'll start running a fever. Then we'll move slower. There's more chance she won't make it."

Courtney looked over at Reyna and saw that she'd been listening. "Don't worry about me," Reyna said vehemently. "I'm going to be strong for us. You'll see." She started struggling up, pressing her back against the face of the cliff for balance. Courtney ran over to help her because she didn't want Reyna to hurt herself. She got her friend standing upright, but swaying slightly like she was light-headed.

Reyna leaned on her and looked at the bundle where her hand had once been. "I got my hand cut off so we could survive." She looked up at Courtney, her dark eyes just a few inches away. "If I got through that, I can get through anything." Her voice was filled with angry pride. "We have to leave soon. We have to."

Her hard-core intensity was unnerving. Courtney continued holding her, helping to bear Reyna's weight. This girl can barely stand, is what she thought. *How is she going to walk more than a few steps at a time?*

Courtney gazed around at her surroundings. There were no birds in the trees, no green signs of life. It was a desolate, abandoned wasteland. A graveyard. The only living things they'd encountered had been the wolves—and the wolves had nearly killed them. Fortunately, they hadn't heard any baying sounds recently, but Courtney didn't doubt the wolves were still out there. Even nature itself was antagonistic. Courtney hoped that between her, Reyna, and J.G., there might be just enough willpower to conquer this miserable place. She gestured toward Jeremy, up on the cliff. "What about him?"

"He's going soft," J.G. said, as he gazed at Jeremy's huddled figure in seeming contempt. "In prison, he'd get turned out and become someone's punk."

"He's scared," Courtney added. J.G. kept his face blank. "This nightmare was too much for him."

"Maybe I should talk to him," Reyna said. "Maybe I can help."

J.G. shrugged. "He better not slow us down."

It seemed callous to Courtney that they were talking about Jeremy—one of her good friends—as though he were some stranger who wasn't even there. But Jeremy wasn't acting like the person they knew, so there wasn't any sense pretending that he was okay.

J.G. walked over to where Courtney and Reyna were standing. Courtney had noticed that since his handcuffs had come off, his lithe body moved slightly differently, more freely. Maybe it was just because he wasn't constrained anymore, but he seemed a little more confident, arrogant even. Courtney hoped it was just elation at being freed. "We need to get back up that cliff and hit the road," J.G. continued. "I'll help both you girls up."

It was surprisingly easy for Courtney, J.G., and even Reyna to get back up to the top of the cliff. The rocks and snow made it simple to find purchases for their feet and hands. To Courtney's relief, it seemed as though Reyna would still be able to hike after all. She had no idea if Reyna's energy would be there six miles from now, though, or even if she would have any energy herself. The cold, the lack of sleep and food, and the brutal physical conditions had sapped her strength and made her want to lie down and give up. But she didn't.

At the top of the cliff, they confronted Jeremy. They

stood around him as he continued to sit there like part of the landscape, looking off into space.

"Jer, we have to leave now," Reyna insisted, holding her injured arm to her chest. "Are you hearing me?"

He nodded aimlessly. "Sure thing," he said, but he made no move to get up.

"Reyna's free," Courtney said, thinking maybe it would help to spell things out for him. "Now we can get to Pine Valley. We need to take Reyna to a hospital, and send people to find Harris and Mel, remember?" She'd stopped thinking about Melanie and Harris herself, but thought maybe their names would jog his memory.

He turned his vacant, wounded eyes to hers. "I'm not ready."

"Too bad," Reyna said tiredly. "This isn't about you."

"Do you want to get left behind?" J.G. asked him. "Because that's what's going to happen if you don't get your shit together." Courtney caught a glimpse of J.G.'s lacerated wrists. They looked swollen and infected, and she realized he probably needed a doctor too.

Jeremy waved his hand wanly in J.G.'s direction. "What do you know about anything?"

"He knows how to help us survive," Courtney told Jeremy.

"Think of what you're missing," Reyna said. "Just a short walk away is warmth, water, and food. That sounds good, right?"

Jeremy sighed and slowly began to get up from the snow. "This trip sucks," he muttered, sounding a little closer to normal but still far from useful. He rubbed his eyes, like a child awakening from a dream, as he stood up. Then he glanced around, took a stumbling step forward, and added, "What are you guys waiting for?"

Courtney breathed an inward sigh of relief that Jeremy was on his feet again. She shared looks with Reyna and J.G., and then they followed after him.

J.G. soon took his usual lead position, guiding them forward in the direction of the town. They walked through the same forest that had seemed so ominous the night before. Now to Courtney it just seemed depressing and exhausting.

Soon they found the road again and continued trudging along it. It still looked untouched—no traffic or signs of activity, just snow on the ground. Courtney and the others moved at a slow but steady pace. The grade of the road was steeper here, and it was difficult for Courtney to keep her legs moving. She was surprised that Reyna was doing so well, considering what had happened to her.

The cold was so intense, Courtney felt like it was inside her bones, trickling up and down like a living creature. She'd never thought that she could feel so cold. She told herself it was good that she could still feel something. She flexed her fingers, clenching them into fists as she walked to get the blood flowing. She could no longer shake the numbness in them, and when she'd examined her fingers earlier they'd looked like they were made of wood.

"Why hasn't someone found us yet?" Jeremy asked plaintively from the back of the line. It wasn't really a question for any of them to answer, Courtney realized, but a cry from his heart for someone to rescue them. "Why are we still out here?"

"Because that's how it is," Reyna said. She was speaking in tight bursts, as though it took a lot of energy to get the words out.

"No one's coming," J.G. called back to Jeremy. "It's better if you just accept that. Makes the journey easier."

"I don't see how," he replied.

"It makes it easier on me, because then I don't have to listen to your complaining." J.G. spat into the snow as he walked, a reflex action, like he'd been chewing tobacco. Courtney suddenly thought it was a stupid thing for him to do, because they needed to conserve the water in their bodies. They were all dehydrated. But then she realized that if any of them were strong enough to make it out of the forest, it would be J.G., so she probably didn't have to worry about him.

If anything, since he'd crawled out of the snow three nights ago, it seemed as though he'd been gaining strength. There was something strange about that, but Courtney didn't know why, and she didn't want to obsess about it. She just wanted to be safe and out of the cold.

"So we're going the right way?" she asked, seeking confirmation that J.G. still knew what he was doing.

"Yup." J.G. nodded. "We'll be turning off the road in a

couple miles or so. That's when it'll get really tough. Steep terrain. Probably some ice slicks on the ground."

"Fantastic," Jeremy muttered. Neither Courtney nor Reyna responded. They just kept plugging ahead.

Two solid hours of walking later, they reached the path that led off the main road and into the forest, like some kind of wayward artery. The trees thinned out, providing an opening at the edge of the snow-covered road. By that point, Courtney could tell Reyna was barely hanging on, because her face was twisted into a mask of pain. In addition, Jeremy was clutching his stomach and moving as though every step was agony.

Courtney felt just as bad. Look at us, she thought. *We're like a bunch of old cripples.* She laughed bitterly in her head, picturing a scorecard that read, Humans: 0, Nature: 1. It was clear that the home team was winning.

"You sure this is it?" Courtney asked, gasping the words as they reached the opening in the trees where the path was. J.G. stopped.

"Ninety-nine percent." He crouched down, eyeing the trail.

Reyna shut her eyes. "What if you're wrong?"

"Let's pretend I'm not."

Courtney gazed up the snowy path. It seemed to ascend a short hill and then veer upward steeply to the right. She could see the tips of boulders peeking out from the heavy snow. It looked like a difficult and dangerous journey.

A few miles of this and we're all going to collapse and

die, she thought glumly. *The whole journey is going to have been in vain.* Then she pushed the thoughts out of her mind. She'd been thinking since the accident they might die. It hadn't happened yet, so maybe it wasn't going to.

What would Elliot want her to do? she suddenly thought to herself. She knew it was crazy to be thinking of him now, a dead brother who she'd never known. But he was still her brother, and if there was some sort of afterlife, then maybe he was looking down on her.

Help us, she thought, willing the words to find their way up to him. *Help us make the right decisions and not mess things up any more than we already have.* It was weird to think that Elliot would probably be around J.G.'s age now, if he had lived. But Elliot was frozen forever in time.

"The town's not getting any closer," J.G. said, as he stared down the path. Even he didn't sound too excited about the prospect of plunging into this wilderness. "Better step to it."

Courtney, Reyna, and Jeremy wearily obeyed his instruction.

It was half an hour later, as they traversed the nearly impossible terrain, that J.G. paused and said, "Wait, I see something."

Courtney tried to come to a stop, but it took effort to make her arms and legs cease moving. Her body had become a walking machine, and she felt like she wasn't completely in control of it anymore. Her rubbery legs took several unintentional tottering steps forward, almost slipping in the snow, until she finally made them stop. She stood there shaking, rubbing herself for warmth and waiting for the feeling to return. Reyna and Jeremy seemed too ill to even speak.

"What is it?" Courtney asked J.G. with concern. After the wolves, she knew they couldn't relax and take any chances.

"Light," was all he said, as he stared out into the forest, through the network of dense tree branches.

"What do you mean?"

"A light that shouldn't be there." He pointed. "Way out there."

Reyna raised her head to look. Courtney noticed her eyes were ringed with black circles.

Courtney suddenly caught a flash of light too, just for an instant, like the reflection of the sun from the windshield of a passing car. Except she knew there was no sun in the dark gray sky, and there were certainly no cars around.

Courtney could tell that J.G. was disturbed by what they were seeing. "What do you think it is?"

"Nothing good."

Jeremy hadn't even bothered to look, but he said, sounding exhausted, "Maybe it's a hunter or something. Maybe they'll help us." Courtney was glad to hear anything remotely optimistic come out of his mouth, but J.G. shut him down.

"There aren't any hunters," J.G. said, still looking into

the trees. Courtney was doing the same thing, but the light didn't come again. "Not in this weather. Not this time of year. Not on this mountain."

"What if it's someone stuck like us?" Courtney asked, her thoughts coming in a rush, but she knew that was fairly unlikely too. No one normal, or smart, would be out here. "What if they sent people to look for us, or for you? Or what if it's a light from Pine Valley?"

"We're too far away from the town," J.G. told her, "and if they send people to look, it'll be in a chopper, not on the ground. Snow's too deep."

Reyna struggled to speak, having seen the light too. "It could be another inmate," she managed to say weakly. "Could be a fire. Does the path take us that way?"

"Close to it, sure," J.G. said. His voice was abruptly nervous.

"Leonard Bell," Courtney said to J.G. "That's who you think the light might be coming from. That he's still out here." J.G. didn't respond, but Courtney knew in her gut it was what he thought. "I'm right, aren't I?"

"Maybe," he admitted.

"Look," Reyna said, pointing shakily with her good arm. Courtney turned and saw the light again. A second later, it blinked off. This time it had come from a slightly different direction from the first time. It hadn't looked like a reflection, either. It had looked like some kind of very bright torch or flashlight.

Courtney doubted anyone would be out there waiting

Alex McAulay

to aid them, but she still had hope. "Maybe it's a cabin with supplies or something. A place for emergencies?" No one answered, so she said, "Or not."

"I wouldn't bet money on it," J.G. finally told her.

"Places like that do exist," Courtney said, wanting to protect her last vestige of hope.

"Not out here."

Reyna staggered a little. Courtney thought she might fall, and took a step toward her, but then Reyna recovered. "I think we should follow the light," she said. "We can sneak up, at least get a look. I need help really bad." Courtney could see a desperate fear in Reyna's eyes, behind her layers of self-control. It made Courtney feel more afraid, both for Reyna and for herself. Reyna was finally acknowledging that she couldn't press on much farther. Her T-shirt bandages were soaked with blood. "If it's a place with supplies, or has a phone, then we have to try. If it's not . . . then we keep going."

"Agreed," Courtney said.

Jeremy was mute, but J.G. nodded at last and said, "Okay. I'm up for a detour. But we better watch our backs."

Courtney looked out toward where the blinking light had been. There was only one way to find out what it really was. "C'mon," she said, dragging her limbs forward. The group began to walk again, the thick snow crunching under their weary feet as they headed toward an unknowable destination. Courtney didn't know whether to be relieved or terrified.

XVIII

By the time Courtney realized that they had all made a horrible mistake, it was almost too late. They were just coming up the crest of a small ridge, making their way through the thigh-deep snowdrifts and occasional underbrush. Right when she came over the top, Courtney saw exactly what they'd stumbled upon. It was a dreamlike image, as though it had been transplanted from another place altogether, or from some bucolic turn-of-the-century oil painting.

Below her and the others stretched a shallow valley. The trees were sparser here, which afforded them a better view of the white landscape. Parallel to them, along the base of the valley, someone had cut a path through the snow, a narrow swath that led to a tiny clearing about twenty yards away.

In the clearing was a large, well-tended fire, nearly smokeless. The blinking light must have been coming from its reflection on the snow. Several feet from it was an even larger, solid-looking snow shelter, similar to an igloo. It seemed to have been constructed with great love and care, and the snow was flattened and packed densely, making it look like it was covered in stucco. Lying around the fire, drying, were some clothes and other unidentifiable objects. Fresh boot prints were everywhere in the clearing.

J.G., Reyna, and Courtney nearly stumbled into one another. Only Jeremy kept moving, and J.G. had to grab him roughly by the shoulder to make him stop. Jeremy started to blurt something in surprise, but everyone hissed at him to shut up.

Courtney had recognized the clothes that were drying in the clearing right away. They were the unmistakable missing uniform of the prison guard. She felt goose bumps running up and down her arms, as she thought two words: *Leonard Bell.* There could be no doubt as to whose campsite this was.

So J.G. had been right all along, Courtney thought. Part of her, deep down, had hoped maybe Leonard wasn't real, or that they would never run into him even if he was. She looked over at J.G. and realized they were all looking at him for guidance, and out of terror. But he was staring down at the campsite, eyes riveted.

"He's in there," J.G. said softly. There was no need for Courtney or anyone to ask who the "he" was.

"In where?" Jeremy replied stupidly. Courtney pointed at the snow shelter, not daring to speak.

"Oh." Jeremy sank to the snow. Courtney, Reyna, and J.G. followed him, ducking down so they weren't visible except for their heads.

Reyna was now scanning the campsite as she held her wounded arm. "How do you know he's there?"

"From the pattern of footprints," J.G. said. "They're fresh. He just went inside—I can tell these things from my army training. He's holed up, most likely with the rifle."

"What—" Courtney began. "What is he doing in there?"

"I don't know!" J.G. snapped in an atypically harsh whisper. "Resting? Sleeping? Jerking himself off? Maybe he's waiting for us to come find him."

"We need to go back to the trail," Reyna said, and Courtney agreed before J.G. could say anything else. She didn't like the way he was looking: ugly and some-how different from before. It was as though encountering Leonard's campsite was bringing out another side of him, the prison side, perhaps.

"We have to get out of here," Courtney told him.

"That won't work anymore," J.G. said.

She didn't understand. "Why not?"

"He'll know that we've been here."

"Not if we don't go down to the campsite," Courtney pointed out.

"He can sense us," J.G. insisted, sounding a little irrational. "He'll survey his perimeter later on, and he'll see our prints. He'll know we came here, and then he'll come after us, for our supplies."

"We don't have any supplies!"

"We have more than he does, and he wants everything he can get."

Reyna finally spoke again, her voice raspy. "I don't buy this bullshit, J.G." It sounded like she was finding it increasingly hard to breathe. "Leonard's not superhuman, am I wrong? He doesn't have magical powers." Another pause. "I'm not even sure he's in that igloo thing. I don't—" Her words broke off in a coughing fit.

"It's your funeral," J.G. said, looking at her blandly. "You don't know him. Some people have special talents for things. Leonard's talent is killing people, hunting them. If you underestimate him, you will get slaughtered like a pig. This is a man who massacred his own family, who ate human flesh."

Reyna was still coughing, so Courtney said to J.G., "What are you saying we should do? You say we can't leave, that he knows we're here. But we can't stay, or he's going to kill us?" She felt a mounting sense of dread and desperation. "You're not making sense."

"We only have one option now." J.G. sounded firm and militaristic, like he couldn't be swayed.

"And that is?"

"We go after him. We get him before he gets us."

"You're serious?" Courtney asked.

"Deadly."

"I thought you were scared of him," Courtney dared to say.

"I'm scared of turning my back on him. Face-to-face, it's just another fight."

"This isn't prison, J.G.," Reyna managed, her coughing fit subsiding. "We're not going to fight your battles for you. We just want to get safe."

"I'm telling you, he'll know we've been here, and he'll hunt us down for sport. Leonard isn't like other people. He's insane. He's like . . . the devil."

"So what do you want us to do?" Courtney asked, equal parts scared and frustrated at J.G. He had definitely been more friendly when he still had his cuffs on.

J.G. turned to her, his eyes clear and cold. "Give me the hatchet. I'll take care of the rest."

"You're going to kill him," Reyna said. It wasn't a question.

"Like you said, you're not going to fight my battles for me. I'll fight them on my own. Leonard left me to die in the cold. He wanted me to suffer."

"That doesn't mean you need to retaliate."

Without hesitation, J.G. said, "Scores were made to be settled."

The idea of murder had always been a very abstract thing to Courtney, but now here it was, staring her in the face. She hadn't thought J.G. would turn out to be so crazy. "Can't we just let him be?" she asked, staring out at the igloo and the campground. It was oddly peaceful down there, even if it was, in fact, the supposed lair of a serial killer.

No one answered her question, perhaps because there was no easy answer, but Reyna said to J.G., "We're not giving you the hatchet." She spoke through her exhaustion and pain. "I'm sorry, there's no way."

"You didn't have any objections when I was helping you," he said. His voice sounded taut, like a rattlesnake coiled before striking. Courtney had the feeling that any second he would flip out and begin screaming at them, or worse. "Besides, you can't really stop me, now can you?"

Reyna tilted her head to one side, as though she were in debate class. "You can't have our hatchet to go murder someone. And that's really what you want to do, isn't it? Not just hurt him but actually kill him."

"Only one way to find out."

"You told us you weren't a murderer," Courtney pointed out. "I thought you were better than that. I believed in you."

"Well, maybe I'll just make it so he can't follow us. Even the odds up a little."

Courtney knew he was lying. Her despair made her feel oddly carefree and momentarily courageous, like it was okay to speak out against J.G. "We shouldn't have cut those handcuffs off you," she said.

"You did it because you needed me."

"You needed us just as badly." Courtney was struck by the futility of it all, of their situation and their petty arguments. Horror was giving way to a mental blankness that matched the numb sensation in her hands and feet.

Jeremy must have been feeling the same way, because he suddenly held out the hatchet, handle first, toward J.G. "Take it," he muttered, the exhaustion making his speech thick and slurred. Courtney moved forward, but J.G. was faster. The prisoner's arms snapped out as he lunged for the weapon.

"No—" Reyna began, but the hatchet was already in J.G.'s hands before she could get another word out of her mouth.

"Thanks," J.G. said to Jeremy, although he was looking at Reyna. For the first time on their journey since he'd come out of the snow at the SUV, Courtney thought that J.G. looked truly scary.

"Just do it already," Jeremy told J.G., "so we can keep moving." He wiped his nose on his sleeve, leaving thick strands of mucus there. "I don't give a flying fuck."

"You shouldn't have done that, Jer," Reyna said to him angrily. She was clutching her injured arm, as though losing the argument over the hatchet had made her wound hurt more. "That was really stupid. What the hell's wrong with you?"

Courtney knew that just a few days ago, such an indictment from Reyna would have made Jeremy tumble all over himself to apologize. But now he barely responded to her words, as though the cold and the stress had chiseled away some core part of him.

"Give it back," Reyna said to J.G. firmly. Courtney contemplated trying to grab the hatchet away from him, but it seemed too dangerous.

J.G.'s face was placid in victory. "Too late for tears now," he told Reyna. "What's done is done." He was clutching the hatchet by its handle, letting the stained blade hang down over the snow. The weapon looked different in his hands from when he'd performed the amputation. Now it somehow looked more dangerous, Courtney thought, and far more lethal.

"You don't have to do this," Courtney pleaded. "Pine Valley's only a few miles away. We can make it home without hurting anyone unless we have to. If we move fast, even if Leonard does start stalking us, we'll have a big lead."

"We can't move fast enough," he retorted. "That's the problem." He gestured at Reyna, and then at Jeremy. "Can they move fast?" His words hung in the air. "If it was just me it might be different, but it's not. A group can never move as fast as an individual. If I take Leonard out, it'll save us all." He looked down at the campsite. "Believe me, if anyone deserves to be taken out, it's him."

His words might have made some small degree of sense, but they were subverted by the manic look in his eyes and the fact that he was gripping the hatchet. Courtney and Reyna looked to Jeremy for support, but he was staring wanly at a snowdrift, like he'd crawled into his own mind and wasn't coming out anytime soon.

Courtney realized they could threaten to leave, but they needed J.G. far more than he needed them. Without him, they wouldn't be able to find the town. And what if the wolves were still after them? Courtney thought. Without J.G., they would be easy prey.

Courtney tried to tell herself that maybe Leonard deserved it, that J.G. was right about everything. But it seemed doubtful Leonard would even know they'd been there, which meant that attacking him with a hatchet while he slept would be a pointless, horrific, and immoral act. It occurred to Courtney that she and Reyna could yell out a warning to the slumbering man in the igloo, but that might mean a death sentence for themselves, from Leonard or even from J.G. himself.

J.G. shouldered the hatchet, preparing for action. "Wait here, behind this ridge. I'll be back soon. You'll be safe up here."

"If you cared about our safety, you wouldn't have put us in this position," Reyna told him.

"Then maybe I don't care that much, okay?" he hissed. "Just stay put and don't make noise."

With those final words, he was gone, practically leaping down the hillside with the hatchet in one hand, an escaped convict with a murder weapon. In an instant he was out from the snowbanks and into the near edge of the clearing. He moved quickly, faster than Courtney could have imagined possible given the crushing hunger, thirst, and fatigue they'd all endured. She realized he would reach the igloo soon and it would be over,

235

one way or another. Reyna and Jeremy were both watching too: Reyna with an intense look of fear, Jeremy with a glassy-eyed stare.

Courtney just had time to whisper to Reyna, "I'm really fucking scared!" before the carnage began.

J.G. reached the opening to the igloo, still silent, and lunged inside with the hatchet. He disappeared from view, except for his feet. He began to scream and rave right as they heard the hatchet come down for the first blow. He wasn't even saying any words, Courtney noted, it was just a mindless, almost gleeful incantation of pure energy. It sounded animalistic, and shattered the tranquility of the barren landscape.

Courtney wasn't even sure there was a person inside the igloo until she heard desperate babbling screams underneath the noises J.G. was making.

Oh God, make this stop, she thought to herself, but things only got worse from there.

They heard grunting and scraping sounds as though the two men were locked in combat. Part of the icy snow enclosure suddenly collapsed, and the other man managed to partially claw his way out, as J.G. struggled to get in more blows.

Courtney could see the other man clearly now. There was no doubt it was Leonard, exactly as J.G. had described him, wearing a prison jumpsuit. He was huge and muscular, with a shaved head and a barrage of tattoos to rival J.G.'s collection. J.G. had obviously already hit him across the head, because the man was bleeding down his face, and a flap of skin was hanging loose, as though he'd been partially scalped.

"No! No!" he was screaming as he tried to get away. His voice was high-pitched like a young girl's, because of his fear. He swiveled his torso around, trying to get at J.G. and the hatchet, but J.G. swung again, the blade narrowly missing Leonard's face and gouging a trough in the snow.

Jeremy was crouching down, his back to the ridge, not even watching. His lips were moving quickly as though he were lost in prayer. But Courtney and Reyna were both standing up, in surprise and shock, absorbing every detail. For some reason Courtney hadn't thought the attack would be this brutal, or that J.G. had this in him—and she hadn't expected Leonard to fight back so hard. She hadn't even thought about what would happen if J.G. lost the fight.

To her horror, as she watched, Leonard looked up in their direction. He saw her and Reyna watching him from above, and he reached out a hand in their direction. "Help me!" he screamed. "Help!" Blood and gore ran down his face in crooked rivulets. J.G. prepared for another blow, but Leonard rolled over on one side and kicked J.G. in the stomach, knocking him into the snow. Leonard managed to get to his knees before J.G. rallied with the hatchet and brought it down again, the blade flat, across Leonard's flank, making the man howl in pain and collapse.

Courtney found herself immobilized by fear, and a

grisly, visceral fascination. Watching J.G. and Leonard struggle over the hatchet was like watching two wolves attacking each other to the death. The movement of the men was a macabre dance. Courtney and Reyna watched in horrified silence as the battle continued. Leonard was much larger than J.G., but he was no match for the hatchet. Courtney just hoped J.G. would end it soon.

J.G. got in another blow, and it split a wedge of flesh in the fatty underside of Leonard's raised arm. J.G.'s face contorted into a rictus of rage and exertion. The dark part of him had taken over, Courtney realized, and the controlled, disciplined man she had come to know over the past few days was no longer in the driver's seat.

As J.G. brought the hatchet down repeatedly, Leonard continued to crawl forward in the snow, vainly attempting to fend off the blows.

Leonard also continued to implore Courtney and her friends for help, his words becoming one long, insistent litany: *"Please, God help me, do something, help me! Fuck, he's gonna kill me!"* To Courtney's ears it sounded bizarrely like a chant. His words got no response. None of them could take the risk of trying to help him, even if they wanted to. Everything felt oddly preordained.

The hatchet came down again, carving additional swaths of red into Leonard's writhing figure. Courtney knew that no matter what Leonard had done, there was no way he deserved such a fate. *How did things come to this?*

Leonard reached out a hand toward them again, trying to grasp across the distance of cold air and reach them. Then he fell facedown in the snow, and J.G. delivered a final blow, the hatchet whisking down and landing with a gritty crunch in the base of Leonard's skull.

After that was silence. Leonard's body was completely still, and Courtney knew the man was dead. The snow all around his body was red, and there was a bloody trail leading all the way back to the collapsed igloo. She looked away for a moment, into the whiteness of the trees. The whiteness was like a blank canvas, and it terrified her. She could get lost in the whiteness forever, and maybe never get out.

Courtney felt an arm on her shoulder and realized it was Reyna.

"I'm going to throw up," Reyna said faintly. Then she did, staggering and bending over at the waist.

Courtney rubbed Reyna's back. Jeremy was sitting down in the snow, his eyes shut. Courtney no longer felt angry at his inability to cope. She knew that every person had some kind of breaking point, herself included. For whatever reason, Jeremy had reached his psychological limit before Courtney or Reyna, but she knew they were not far behind him.

She looked back down at the bloody scene and saw J.G. heading toward them. He had the hatchet in one hand, and a rifle—presumably the one Leonard had taken from the guard—in the other. He was also carrying a large loop of rope that he had found near the guard's uniform. Leonard, or what was left of him, was still there in the snow. Courtney was very scared of J.G. now, yet she had the curious feeling that he wouldn't hurt her. In fact, maybe he'd saved them all by killing Leonard, even if it didn't feel that way and she wished he hadn't done it.

Courtney and Reyna did not run as J.G. approached. But when he reached them, climbing the small rise to where they were, Courtney unconsciously flinched and shied away from him. He didn't seem to notice or care. His clothes were bloody and he was breathing hard, but he brushed right past her and Reyna. He stood a few paces behind them, still holding his weapons. Courtney turned to face him.

"It's over," he said gruffly, not looking at her or anyone. "Let's go."

When he raised his head, she glanced away immediately, scared to make eye contact with him again. Yet in that moment, she thought she saw something that truly terrified her: J.G. appeared to be smiling.

"It was self-defense," J.G. quickly asserted, as Courtney's pulse pounded. By the sound of his voice, she could tell he wasn't smiling anymore. But had he noticed that she'd seen it? Had Reyna or Jeremy seen it too? No one disagreed with J.G. now, because no one dared to. "I had to neutralize him. The best offense is a good defense." Silence. "Okay, let's go," he finally said, annoyed. His face was hard again. "We're hitting the trail, so get Jeremy to stand the fuck up. We only got a few klicks left."

Courtney nodded dumbly, still trying to process what

she'd seen. *After all the sickening violence, what had that smile meant?* She was very much aware that J.G. still had the bloody hatchet in his hands. He'd slung the rifle over his shoulder.

Jeremy finally got to his feet, staggering a little and moaning.

"Saddle up," J.G. told them as he wiped the hatchet blade in the snow.

Slowly, Courtney and the ragged group of travelers began moving through the forest again.

XIX

The next few hours of hiking, along the side of the mountain, were over some of the roughest terrain they'd encountered so far. In a way, Courtney was glad, because it took her mind off the atrocity she'd witnessed back at Leonard's campsite. What J.G. had done was truly abhorrent, even if it was necessary.

Courtney didn't want to examine the implications of her own actions too much. What did it mean that she had stood there and done nothing while a man pleaded for his life? What, if anything, did it say about her? Even if it had been exactly the right thing to do, why did it feel wrong? There was no training for this kind of situation, not in school, or in church, or from her mom and dad. She was alone in it.

The grade of the slope became steeper, so walking

grew even more difficult and perilous. They were gradually ascending the gentle incline of the mountain. Sometimes Courtney felt like she was falling asleep on her feet, while her body continued to walk. She'd fade out for a second, and then snap awake a moment later, still walking. Reyna was stumbling along next to her, or sometimes a few paces behind, with Jeremy bringing up the rear. J.G. continued to lead the pack.

Courtney had lost all sense of place and time. She didn't ask J.G. how far they were from Pine Valley now, partly because she was scared of talking to him, and partly because she just didn't want to know. She knew the only way to get there was to walk, so it didn't matter if they were one mile away or several. She was learning that survival didn't take any particular sort of courage, just brute perseverance against odds that frequently seemed insurmountable.

Often her thoughts drifted back to her life before the accident: to her parents, to school, to her friends and to everyday events. She hadn't felt particularly happy back then, but now those memories were suffused with a rosy glow. She would give anything to get back to her normal, mundane routines. Things that had seemed so upsetting and brought her down—like her breakup with Chris, or her crush on Jeremy—now seemed completely trivial. *What did one boy even matter?* She wondered why she'd ever cared so much in the first place. She was the one who should matter most to herself.

It was easier to think about the past than to focus on

the present. She didn't want to dwell too much on what she'd seen J.G. do to Leonard, although the gruesome images of violence kept coming back to her unbidden. J.G.'s sudden, inexplicable smile was perhaps worst of all, and it cast serious doubt on his character, even more than the murder did. She wondered what he would do when they got to Pine Valley. They had all seen him commit cold-blooded murder, justified or not. Wasn't he concerned they would tell the police? Did he expect them to back him up? She had a bad feeling about things.

"Step it up!" J.G. barked like a drill instructor, turning back to look at them. "You're slowing down."

"I can't . . . I'm tired," Jeremy moaned from behind.

"We're all tired. You can rest when we get there." J.G. kept plowing forward again, even faster.

Reyna stumbled and Courtney had to help her along, grabbing hold of her and pulling her through the snow. Reyna's breathing sounded weird, so Courtney said, "Rey, are you okay?"

Reyna could barely speak, but she managed to nod. "I'm doing really great," she answered between gritted teeth.

Courtney almost laughed. Was Reyna making a joke? Courtney's urge to laugh turned into a roiling sensation of panic and nausea. "Let me know if you need help," Courtney managed.

"Don't you worry about me," Reyna replied, her voice little more than a whisper, but it had some bite to it.

Courtney was relieved that the amputation and all the torments they'd suffered so far hadn't damaged her friend's spirit. She looked up ahead at the white terrain stretching in all directions between the trees like a choppy, frozen ocean.

"J.G.," she called out to the figure striding several paces in front of her.

"What?" he called back, without even bothering to turn around or stop moving. Since killing Leonard, he seemed filled with a new kind of energy, or perhaps mania. It was like he'd got yet another second wind.

"We'll be there soon, right?"

"Yup," he said back. It wasn't exactly the confident answer she was looking for.

I hope J.G. knows where he's taking us, she thought. They had no option but to continue trusting him, even though Courtney couldn't get over that secret smile. She knew he hadn't intended for her to see it.

They continued their long walk, stopping for brief rests, until the sun lowered in the sky and the day slouched toward twilight. Whenever Courtney looked up, the sky above no longer held clouds in it. But it also didn't have any helicopters or airplanes in it either, or anything that could see or rescue them. Where is everyone? she wondered dully. *They have to know something's wrong by now. Why aren't they out here looking for us?*

It was only as the sky grew darker that J.G. finally stopped hiking, leaning down against the hatchet for balance. Courtney was glad to see that he was getting tired too.

"We have to make camp again," he said. "Build another shelter. Start a fire. Keep watch." Courtney thought he sounded bored by the litany. "You know the drill."

"We're supposed to be out of here by now," Jeremy said, leaning against a tree. Courtney was surprised to hear him speak up. "You said we'd make it to town."

"I never said that. I said Pine Valley was nearby, that's all." He rubbed one of his wrists as he played with the hatchet, digging it deeper into the snow. "In this kind of weather? It could take an extra day."

"Yes, but, you said—" Jeremy began, and then he broke off, tears in his eyes. "You said . . ."

Reyna sat down in the snow. She held her wrapped stump gingerly in front of her face, inspecting it.

"We're not lost, are we?" Courtney asked, voicing her worst fear.

J.G. shook his head. "We'll get there tomorrow, I guess." There was a note of finality in his voice, like he was saying, *This topic of conversation is now closed.*

Reyna lowered her arm. "What are you going to do when we get there, J.G.? I mean, when we reach town?" She sounded like she was choosing her words carefully.

"What do you mean?"

"I mean, are you still going to turn yourself in?" She held his gaze.

"Sure," he said after a beat.

"Really." Reyna sounded skeptical. Courtney didn't know where she was headed with this line of questioning, but she wished that Reyna would shut up. Reyna didn't know about the smile. "Aren't you worried we'll"— Reyna paused to cough—"that we'll say something about what you did to Leonard Bell?"

J.G.'s eyes narrowed slightly, but other than that, he didn't have much of a reaction. "Leonard was self-defense. Strategic self-defense." He straightened his back. Courtney could see the barrel of the rifle sticking up over his shoulder. "Everyone knows Leonard was psychotic. I did society a favor. Besides, it's better to be judged by twelve than carried by six, if you get what I mean." He turned away from them and said, "Now let's dig in for the night and get that fire started."

Not knowing what else to do, Courtney and the others slowly obeyed. They were now essentially his prisoners.

It was later that night, crammed together in their hastily constructed snow shelter, that Courtney obsessively worried about J.G.'s motives. His nonchalance about getting to town seemed forced. He no longer seemed humble and frightened, like he had at first, like all of them were. Maybe he had plans to ditch them right before they got to town and run off, Courtney mused. It just seemed so unlikely to her that he'd turn himself back over to the authorities. Her thoughts turned darker—perhaps he was planning on killing them before they reached the town. After all, he had more than enough weapons. Yet so far he'd helped them more than hurt them, and he was continuing to help, even if his manner had turned brusque. Maybe she'd been mistaken about his smile; maybe he'd been trying to fight back tears or something—but she doubted it.

Courtney knew if she were rested she'd be able to puzzle things out more clearly, but she was so tired and cold that her mind was fuzzy. Her throat was raw from dehydration, and it felt like her stomach lining was eating itself. Sleep overtook her quickly in the snow cave that night, as a way for her body to escape the pain, and despite the intense cold—or perhaps because of it—she was soon deep in a dream.

Hours later she was awake again, jolted from sleep by a strange sensation on her neck. She thought some ice from the enclosure must have fallen down into her jacket, and she tried to swipe it away. Instead, her hand touched something hard and unyielding. Confused and scared, she opened her eyes.

Before she could scream, a cold, rough hand covered her mouth, smothering her. She fought back against it, biting the leather glove as the hand squeezed her jaw tightly, and trying to push against the body that had appeared in front of her.

In terror, she realized it was J.G. He was crouched there, a dark shape blocking the opening to the ice shelter. His other hand was pressing the hatchet blade against her throat.

"Don't move. Don't speak," he told her. His voice was

low and quite calm. For an instant Courtney thought she must still be dreaming, or maybe hallucinating, but the blade was pinching her throat and the pain was all too real. "You've done enough talking. You and your friends. Now you're going to listen."

Courtney heard a low moaning sound of fear and realized it was coming from deep inside her. She couldn't believe what was happening. Even after all the signs, she never thought J.G. would actually do this. She tried to press herself back against the wall of the shelter, to get away from the blade, but there was nowhere to go. Stay calm, stay calm, she told herself, but she felt her sanity slipping away. *What is he going to do to me?*

This could be how my life ends, she thought. *Right here and now, in this dark, cold moment, miles from home.* She realized then it was just her and J.G. in the shelter—Reyna and Jeremy were gone somewhere. Maybe they were already dead. She might now die alone too. She felt disbelief and horror that in the end, it had come down to this.

"I'm not going to hurt you," J.G. continued, although the hatchet at her neck belied his words. "I could cut off your head if I wanted, but I won't do that." She could feel his breath warm on her neck in the freezing air. "I like you."

Courtney tried to scream, but J.G. gouged his gloved fingers into her cheeks, locking her mouth shut, and said, "Shhh."

Courtney was crying. She wanted to ask, *Why are*

you doing this? How the fuck could you? But she realized the question didn't have any satisfactory answer.
J.G. was a convicted prisoner, a murderer, and probably
crazy. And they had trusted him. Now he could do whatever he wanted.

"You're never going to see Reyna again," he continued. "I'm taking her with me where I'm headed. I've
already got her outside, ready to go. Jeremy's out there
too. You'll see him again, though." He played with the
hatchet blade, moving it back and forth a little, up and
down. "I'm leaving him behind for you." Courtney knew if
J.G. exerted enough pressure on the blade, it would
break the skin. "I've been on the fence about you, Courtney. I almost took you instead of Reyna. But she's
smaller, weaker, and she's only got one hand. It will be
harder for her to fight back. . . ." His words were delivered in a terrifyingly banal tone of voice.

Courtney couldn't speak, but she mouthed one word:
"Why?"

In the gray light, the darkness before dawn, she saw
him smile again. "This is the way it has to be," he said. "It
never could have been any other way. All choices led to
this moment." He shifted the weight of his crouching
body, but held the hatchet blade firm. "You never had a
chance. This is your fate, and this is my fate. This is the
fate of your friends."

Courtney felt the blade press tighter. It made her feel
like something was caught in her throat, and she tried
not to gag. She shut her eyes again, feeling the world

reeling around her. Had killing Leonard unleashed some demon inside of J.G. that could no longer be quelled? Or had he planned all this from the start? The blade kept her silent. She couldn't even swallow.

"Don't come after me, and don't send anyone after me," J.G. continued. "You'll never find me. Just continue on to Pine Valley. I don't care what you tell them when you get there. They'll never catch me again. I know these woods better than anyone." He paused. "Keep going east. You'll find a river. Follow it. We're less than two miles from town."

Courtney didn't feel relief; she felt as though she was going to pass out. She also felt a horrible dread, like an abyss opening up inside her, suddenly afraid that J.G. wasn't really going to let her go. That he was going to kill her like he'd killed Leonard, and this was all just some kind of sick prelude.

"Don't hurt me," she tried to say, but she couldn't summon the words. The blade moved on her neck and she started to pray for the end to come quickly, if it came, and not hurt too much. She was more afraid of pain than of death. She heard a rustling sound, like something moving through the air, and in absolute fear she gasped, "Please!" She was afraid he was raising the blade to strike her.

To her surprise, the word rang out loudly in the darkness. Her eyes flew open and she brought a hand up to her neck. The blade was gone, and so was J.G. She was staring out the opening of the snow cave at fading stars

Alex McAulay

in the blue-black sky. The pain in her throat was agonizing, so she tore off her glove and brought it to her neck again. Her hand came back slick with something, and she realized the rough blade had cut her neck just a little. Enough to bleed a bit, but not much else.

I'm alive, she thought, her heart racing and her whole body trembling. *I'm still alive.* Every breath felt like a victory, and she started to sob. She felt angry at herself for crying, but she couldn't make the tears stop. It took several minutes until she was able to climb out of the snow cave and stand up in the frigid open air.

When she got outside, she looked around. There was no sign of J.G. or Reyna, other than fresh tracks leading away from the camp and into the barren wilderness of pines. She listened, trying to hear if Reyna was screaming for help, but the landscape was silent except for the noises of the snow and ice.

When she looked in the other direction, to her left, she saw something slumped in the snow. It took her a second to realize it was Jeremy, with his jacket, hat, and gloves stripped off. She knew she should rush over to him, but something held her back. She had a terrible feeling that Jeremy was no longer alive. She began edging her way over to him, her mind overwhelmed by fear.

When she reached him, she saw that she'd been right. He was lying half curled up on his side, the snow deep red all around him. His throat had been cut. More than cut, in fact. It had been smashed in, so that he was partially decapitated, his trachea demolished. In the

253

instant before she looked away, Courtney could see white splinters of bone sticking out from the wound like toothpicks.

She sat down, stunned into oblivion. It was clear J.G. had done this. There could be no other explanation. J.G. killed Jeremy, she thought, still trying to wrap her head around the idea. *Jeremy is dead. He's not coming back, not ever.* She didn't believe it, even though the evidence was clear. She knew J.G. was a killer, she had seen it with Leonard, but this was very different. Leonard was probably a monster, a killer himself. But she had known Jeremy since ninth grade. They had been friends, and despite herself she had liked him as more than a friend. She wondered why she wasn't crying anymore. She guessed she was probably in a state of shock.

Courtney didn't feel like herself. She felt as though everything was unreal, as if her mind had become unglued from her body. She realized that she was breathing rapidly, unconsciously hyperventilating, and she forced herself to take slower, deeper breaths. The idea that Jeremy was really dead seemed unfathomably huge. She couldn't ever imagine accepting it or getting over it.

He must be cold, she suddenly thought. She knew it was irrational, because he was clearly dead, and dead people didn't feel anything. But she was struck by the urge to warm him up somehow, to cover him. She didn't have anything to put over him, and he was too heavy to drag into the snow cave. Besides, she didn't want to touch his body. It would be as cold and lifeless as the landscape around her, not like the person she'd once known so well.

She wondered why J.G. hadn't used the gun, because the hatchet seemed so much crueler. Then she realized why: he was saving bullets.

Jeremy, Jeremy, she thought, repeating his name in her head as though the invocation might bring him back to life. Somehow through the clutter of her thoughts, a sharp voice cut through. The voice told her that Jeremy was dead, and she would have to deal with it, whether she wanted to or not.

His journey is over, the voice said. *Yours isn't.* The voice came through as clearly as a radio signal broadcast direct from some deep part of her subconscious. *Get your crap together and start walking. Find the town. Save yourself.*

Staring back at Jeremy's corpse, she thought, But what about Reyna? Courtney refused to leave her friend behind.

Forget Reyna, the voice advised. *She's long gone.*

I could go after them, Courtney told the voice. *I could track them down and find her. It's not snowing anymore, so their tracks will be visible. J.G. won't be able to hide from me.*

The voice was unimpressed with her logic. *Please. You'll never find them. You'll just get yourself lost. And even if you did find them, what would you do? J.G. has a gun and a hatchet.*

Courtney didn't have an answer, but the voice did: *J.G. would kill you, like he's killed the others. He is wild. You are tame.*

Courtney stood up, trying to make the voice fall silent. The temptation to head for Pine Valley was unbearable. After all she'd been through, she knew she could make it a couple more miles. Then she could get help there and make them send the police back to find J.G. and Reyna. But she knew it was doubtful they'd ever find Reyna, at least not alive. Too much time would have elapsed, enough time for J.G. to escape for good into the mountains. Courtney knew it would take her hours to make the journey into town, and in that time, J.G. could dig himself in somewhere with Reyna and hide.

With every second that she waited, she knew that J.G. and Reyna were getting farther away from her, and hope was receding. She looked over at Jeremy's body again. There wouldn't even be time to bury him in the snow if she went after them.

"I'll come back for you," she whispered to Jeremy suddenly, knowing he could no longer hear her.

She couldn't really believe the choice she was about to make, but she realized she could not give up and head to Pine Valley. She didn't have it in her. She would go after Reyna.

You're crazy, the voice told her, its tone acidic. *You're going to get yourself killed. Are you so fucking stupid you can't even save your own life when it's handed to you on a silver platter? J.G. let you go—*

"Shut up!" she yelled, willing the awful voice away. You don't know what I'm capable of, she told it silently. *You never have. I'll prove it to you.*

The voice did not respond, but she feared it was girding itself up for another round.

She suddenly remembered Jeremy's journal, and she felt an unreasonable urge to go and get it. She didn't want to waste time, but it felt important to her. If she couldn't bury him, at least she could reunite him with something precious. Everything of value had been taken by J.G., but the journal had been left behind, carelessly discarded in the snow, open at the center with the pages facedown.

She picked up the journal. For a second, she didn't know what she was supposed to do with it after all—whether she should keep it with her or leave it with its author. She wanted to do whatever he would have wanted. She glanced down at the page it was open to and brushed off the snow. Her eyes couldn't help scanning the words written there in scribbly black ink. Reyna's name stuck out to her at once.

"I feel so guilty," she read silently from the page. "I wanted to have more time with her. I am a stupid fucking moron." Those last three words were underlined twice. "I killed all of us. I doomed us—" Here the writing became unintelligible, the pen gouging into the page like the point of a knife. It looked like a lunatic had written it.

Puzzled, she flipped back a few pages, even though she knew she was wasting important time. As her eyes moved across the pages, she began to understand what had gone wrong with Jeremy.

"They'd kill me if they knew," she read to herself. "I told them we hit a deer, but I lost control. I think I fell asleep." And then, a few pages before that, "I wanted to spend more time with Reyna. I took the long way down this road because of her. I didn't know this would happen, but it is ALL MY FAULT, the reason that we're stuck here. Why couldn't I stay awake? I love her. I was going to tell her. I just needed more time . . ."

Courtney closed the book, overwhelmed by emotion. She couldn't believe what she'd just read. She wondered why Jeremy had even dared to write it, but perhaps it had been a necessary cathartic purge. Through the journal, the dead had spoken and confessed. Jeremy had taken the rural route—the "shortcut"— knowing it would take longer, in order to spend more time with Reyna. He clearly blamed himself for everything that had happened after that, especially the accident. Courtney guessed it partly explained his behavior throughout the ordeal: he had been burdened by guilt. Guilt had motivated his actions and slowly enervated him. And in the end he had found the punishment he desired for his imagined sins. J.G. had been his judge, jury, and executioner, without even knowing it.

Now Jeremy was a silent, frozen statue in the snow, his life congealed all around him. All Courtney felt was unendurable sorrow and pity. She decided to leave the book with his body. It was part of him, and it didn't belong with her. She wished he could have shared his secrets with her; then they might not have eaten him away. She understood why he'd lied, but it didn't matter if there'd been a deer or not. The wreck wasn't his fault, it was the fault of the storm. She placed the journal next to him on the snow, his last will and testament.

Courtney went and picked up one of the backpacks. She was going to hoist it over her shoulder, but then she realized it was empty and there was no point in bringing it. She tossed it back down.

Even Courtney didn't think she would really succeed in finding Reyna. But a kind of madness drew her onward. She did not look back as she began to follow J.G.'s and Reyna's footprints in the snow, heading away from safety and deeper into the cold heart of the forest.

XX

For the first mile, Courtney stumbled along, her mind focused solely on her goal of finding Reyna. She was determined not to give up, and to follow the footprints to their inevitable conclusion. She didn't know what she would do when, or if, she caught up with J.G. and Reyna. She wasn't sure there was anything she could do, but she vowed to try. It was down to her now, and she wasn't going to let Reyna die alone.

Courtney wondered whether she might end up dying herself, whether this journey would become a death march or suicide trip. She knew she didn't want to die. Perhaps she was making a stupid decision, blinded by exhaustion and fear, but inside she felt a deep conviction that she was doing the right thing—the *only* thing she could do.

Besides, we made bad decisions all along, she thought. What would one more matter? She realized there had never really been a single dramatic turning point, just multiple bad choices in larger increments, one after another.

Courtney concentrated her thoughts on following the footsteps in the snow. She could easily tell Reyna's footsteps from J.G.'s. His were firm and large, while hers were crooked and uneven. In some places it looked like he'd been dragging her. There were no signs they had stopped to rest. Courtney could only imagine the kind of agony that Reyna might be in. She doubted that J.G. was treating her gently.

Courtney knew she had to think and act dispassionately, or else the force of her emotions would overwhelm her. She tried to ignore the cold, and make her stiff, dehydrated limbs move forward. It was so cold now that any exposed skin was either completely numb or burned with searing pain, as though the air were boiling hot.

I really need a plan, she told herself as she moved through the deep snow. She guessed that she had the element of surprise; she doubted that J.G. expected her to follow them. He would not anticipate such tenacity. But other than that, if she found them, everything else would be in his favor. He had the gun and the hatchet, he had Reyna, and he was stronger than she was. It would take very little effort on his part to overpower her and then kill her, just like he'd done to Jeremy and Leonard. She knew now that J.G. was a madman, and that he was not constrained by the normal boundaries of human conduct. She still didn't know why he hadn't killed her already when he had the chance.

With some surprise, she realized she wasn't afraid anymore, at least not like she'd been at the beginning of their journey. In a weird way, for the first time since the car accident, she felt like she was in control of her own destiny again. Instead of being hunted—by wolves, by Leonard, by J.G.—she had now become the hunter.

She moved low to the ground and as swiftly as she could. Her legs throbbed but she worked to put the pain out of her mind. She continued trying to strategize as she walked, following the seemingly endless pattern of tracks up the steep snowbanks. She was grateful now for all the snow, or else the path would have been lost forever. The footsteps continued in a hypnotic, unbroken chain.

Courtney didn't want to stop hiking, but she was forced to rest at certain points when breathing became too difficult and her thighs cramped and spasmed. Then she would stop and hunch over, desperately rubbing at the muscles and praying for them to relax so that she could continue. Eventually they would, and she'd keep plunging forward again, despite her thirst and exhaustion. She had been so long without food, she didn't feel hunger anymore.

She was certain J.G. would have to stop and make camp at some point, probably when night fell. That meant he would have to forage for wood and build a snow cave, and possibly go to sleep. Any of those actions might provide Courtney with the chance to reach Reyna, assuming her friend was still alive. She hoped she could somehow gain a vantage point on J.G. when he set up camp. Then, if the right opportunity presented itself, she could get to Reyna and flee with her into the forest.

It sounded unlikely, even to her. If they ran, Courtney knew that J.G. would then be able to follow their footprints, just as she was following his. She hadn't quite solved that problem yet, and knew it might not have a solution.

Courtney continued on her nightmare journey. Tiny particles of ice and snow, whipped up off the ground and from the trees by the increasing wind, kept getting in her eyes and sticking there. She had to squint to keep moving. She wished that Jeremy were still alive so she wouldn't feel so alone.

Courtney walked in the tracks left by J.G. and Reyna, sometimes putting her own feet into their impressions. The farther she traveled, the more she observed Reyna's prints becoming a deep, blurred trough, as though the girl could barely walk anymore. Courtney didn't know what shape Reyna would be in when she found her. She'd already lost a hand—could she stay alive much longer?

Sometimes Courtney thought she heard the baying of the wolves faintly in the distance, and their keening, animal voices sent perpetual chills down her back. She

264

didn't want to think about them too much. She guessed that she would probably be safe in the daylight, but she wasn't sure. *Was anything J.G. told us true?* Now that she was by herself, without fire, encountering the wolves might be deadly.

Courtney wondered where J.G.'s and Reyna's tracks were leading. *Perhaps J.G. has some secret destination in mind,* she thought. If he knew the area as well as he claimed, then maybe this was a cut-through to the town, or to some area where he could hide. She saw no indication that any signs of life were nearby.

I have to keep moving, she told herself. *Wherever he's taking her, I will find her.*

It was a prayer, a vow, and most of all, a promise.

Over three hours later, Courtney's expedition came to an unexpected end. The tracks she was following veered sharply to one side, into even deeper foliage. She slowed her pace and moved forward cautiously.

Then she caught a glimpse of something bright in the distance. Unsure of what it was, she stopped walking completely and crouched down on her aching legs. *Is it a trap?* She consulted her gut but got no answer. She realized that the dual set of footprints descended into a tree-lined gully, and that through the white trees, she could see a campsite about forty yards away. There was a small fire and a snow shelter. In addition, something was leaning up against one of the trees near the site.

Her heartbeats echoed loudly in her ears as she realized the footprints ended at the campsite in a morass of churned-up snow. The dark shape against the tree started coalescing into a human form, and Courtney gasped when she realized it was Reyna.

At first she thought Reyna was definitely dead. Her head was hanging down on her chest, and her arms were behind her back, lashed around the tree trunk. She had been tied to the tree somehow, its icy trunk swept bare, and her body tightly affixed so she could not escape.

But as Courtney watched, she saw faint movement and realized with a surge of relief that Reyna was still alive. The girl was straining weakly to get free of her bonds, but was unable to make progress. Her head lolled back down to her chest again.

J.G. was nowhere in sight. Courtney had a terrifying feeling that maybe he knew she was coming after all and was circling back around to get her, so she spun around. She moved so fast she got dizzy, but there was no one behind her. Yet.

She risked another glance back at Reyna. Reyna was motionless again, but at least now Courtney knew she was alive. Courtney was all too aware this could still be a trap set up to lure her in. Yet it was also very likely J.G. was just off doing something routinely mundane, like gathering firewood, or going to the bathroom.

Courtney realized she had two options. The first was to dig in, hide herself, and watch what happened next. She assumed at some point J.G. would inevitably return and tend to the fire. However, it was possible that when he came back, J.G. would kill Reyna, or let her die from exposure to the cold. J.G. hadn't thought twice about killing Jeremy or Leonard, so Courtney knew another life wouldn't matter very much to him. She remembered how he had tended to Reyna, and helped them. Obviously it had all been an act, although she still didn't fully understand why.

Courtney's second option was to take advantage of J.G.'s absence and run down through the trees toward Reyna. There was a chance she could reach her friend, and maybe even free her, before J.G. returned. She knew this course of action was far more dangerous for herself, but she also knew it might be her only chance to save Reyna's life. And together they would be stronger than either of them were right now.

Courtney knew if she thought about it too much, she would lose her nerve, and ultimately the luxury of deciding. J.G. would just come back, and the choice would be made for her. She tried to calm her mind and ignore her panic and exhaustion.

I have to make a decision, she told herself. *I can't delegate the responsibility to someone else, because there is no one else.* There was no one left to make the hard choices for her anymore. She thought about Jeremy's crippling guilt over the accident. It had paralyzed him, and he had died in a paroxysm of self-hatred. Courtney didn't want to die that way.

She stood up. J.G. was still gone, and the path was clear.

I'm going to rescue Reyna, she thought, barely believing it herself.

But before she had time to question her decision, her body was already in motion. From somewhere, a burst of energy erupted, and she tore through the trees down toward the place where Reyna was being held captive. Her heart was caught between her chest and her larynx the whole time, in dread and anticipation. She ran as fast as her damaged, tortured body would allow.

Within thirty seconds she had crashed down into the gully, almost slipping in the snow, and was just fifteen feet away from Reyna. Reyna lifted her head and peered out at her with a dazed expression, as though she thought she was dreaming. Then her mouth formed a perfect O of surprise as she watched Courtney approach.

Courtney got to Reyna's side within an instant and grabbed on to her friend. Reyna was tied to the tree with a rope that looped around her body in thick strands. Courtney could barely look at Reyna because she was so terrified that J.G. would reappear. She kept staring over her shoulders in every direction, her heart pounding.

Courtney started talking to Reyna, barely aware of what she was saying: "I'm getting you out of here! Don't worry. You'll be safe." She was tugging on the rope that bound Reyna, but she couldn't make it give. "Where is he? Where's J.G.?"

Reyna tried to say something as she pulled on Courtney's arm with her good hand. Her face was drawn, and there were frostbitten sores on it.

"Tell me," Courtney said, her voice fraught with fear. She knew that J.G. could be watching them at this very moment.

"The . . . hatchet . . ." Reyna whispered, summoning up what little strength remained inside her. "He left it . . . here . . ."

Courtney swung her head back around. "Where?"

"Behind the snow cave . . ." Reyna tried to speak more words but gagged. Courtney held her head up, all the while feeling the nauseating crush of time pressing in on her. Every second J.G. could be drawing closer. "I don't know where he went. . . . He took the gun. But he left . . . the hatchet . . ."

Courtney looked into Reyna's flagging eyes. "I'll go get it. I'll be right back."

She tore away from her friend, racing through the snow and across the campsite to J.G.'s snow cave. She knew the hatchet would be strong enough to cut through the rope and get Reyna free. After that, they would have to run into the forest and put as much space between them and the campsite as possible before J.G. returned.

Courtney reached the snow cave and skidded forward in the snow, like she was sliding into home base. The snow cave was large and igloo-like, with holes in it, almost like little windows. She realized it was so J.G. could see people approaching when he was inside it. She caught a glimpse of the hatchet's wooden handle behind the shelter, and she reached out and pulled it up and out of the snow. J.G. had wedged it blade-downward, and it came loose in an arc of powder that cascaded back behind her.

Courtney staggered to her feet. She felt safer with the freezing shaft of the weapon in her hand, its hungry blade facing out in front. The hatchet was no match for a rifle, she knew, but it was better than nothing. Reyna remained tied to the tree, watching with frightened eyes. Courtney ran back over to her.

When she got there, Reyna seemed more alert. There was now a small pilot light of hope in her eyes, where before there had been mostly despair.

"Keep still," Courtney instructed as she moved behind the tree and prepared for the first blow.

"I have to tell you something—" Reyna gasped, as Courtney readied herself to swing. "J.G. lied to us this whole time. There were only two convicts in the van that night. Him and one other prisoner. The other prisoner's name—it was J.G." The words were coming out in staccato bursts. "The guy we knew as J.G. is actually Leonard Bell . . . the psychopath. He took the other man's identity. He fooled us. . . ."

Courtney heard the words, but her brain refused to make sense of them. She felt very confused. *J.G. is*

Leonard? She knew if she dwelled on it too much right now she would fail to save Reyna and herself. This was not the time for talking. She put Reyna's words out of her mind and focused on the loops of rope around the tree trunk.

Reyna didn't flinch as Courtney swung the hatchet, catching the rope full on with the blade. But inexplicably, the rope didn't break. The hatchet was now blunt enough from carving through metal and flesh that it just drove the rope deep into the bark.

"Shit!" Courtney hissed, gazing around at the snow, watching in desperation in case J.G. reemerged.

"Hurry," Reyna urged, and Courtney said, "I'm trying!"

She swung again, even harder, but the dull blade just plowed the rope even further into the tree. Reyna gasped in pain as the coils tightened across her body and gouged into her skin.

Courtney took a deep breath and gave a third and final swing. This time the impact was great enough that the rope was severed, and Reyna fell forward into the snow, down to her knees. She crouched in the snow, liberated, holding the stump of her truncated arm up to her chest.

Shaking, Courtney went to Reyna's side and helped her to her feet. "I'm going to pass out," Reyna said woozily, like she was feeling a head rush.

"You can't," Courtney told her. "Or we'll die. You have to stay awake." Her voice had moved beyond pleading or commanding. It was flat and cold, just stating the facts. There was no room for anything else, no room for emotion anymore, only action.

Somehow the words worked, because Reyna nodded and managed to ward off unconsciousness. "Okay."

"We have to run," Courtney said, as she stared out into the forest. "He'll see our footprints, but maybe we can hide somehow."

"We can't hide."

"What? Why?" Courtney asked, her head still trying to wrap itself around the horrific situation.

"Leonard is playing a game with us now. . . . Both prisoners in that van were killers. The other man—the real J.G.—killed the guard, and Leonard ran for it. He saw us, you and me, when we stopped at that storage building, and he followed us back to the SUV." She took a breath. "He used us to survive until we got the handcuffs off him. He used us for food and water, and heat. . . . He was never in the army. Now we're not useful to him anymore, at least not alive. He's going to hunt us down. He's like a mountain man, an animal. He said he can live in the woods forever and disappear from society."

"Jesus . . ."

"He told me—" Reyna broke off, suddenly overcome by fear and disgust. She wiped tears from her eyes. "He said he was going to use me for meat. To live on. After he'd done . . . other things to me. Sex things."

Courtney had no words.

"And then he said he would go after you."

"Listen, we have to run," Courtney said firmly, gripping the hatchet harder. It was insane to stand there talking when he could come back at any minute. "We have to get to Pine Valley before he finds us. We can do it, Reyna. We have to try."

"But don't you see?" Reyna asked, her eyes displaying a flash of wild terror. "There is no town. There never was. Leonard's taken us out into the middle of nowhere to stalk us. We're lost."

XXI

*L*ost. *There is no town.* Courtney almost dropped the hatchet in shock. It hadn't occurred to her, even as Reyna was explaining J.G.'s true identity, that he had been lying about the location of Pine Valley.

All this time we've been going nowhere, she thought to herself bleakly. Getting sicker and colder, and there was no destination. In some ways, it felt like the cruelest betrayal of all.

"Rey, what are we going to do?" she asked. "Why would J.G.—wait, I mean, Leonard—do this?" It was hard to think of "Leonard" as his real name.

"This is what he's good at. Killing. Hunting. He told me that everything he said about Leonard was true . . . but it was really about him. That he killed his own family and cannibalized his sister. That he's killed and hurt many people in his life. That nothing else brings him so much pleasure." She coughed, her chest rattling.

"Leonard's evil," Reyna continued. "Those tattoos . . . I knew he was evil, but I didn't want to believe someone could be like that, not for real. We never should have helped him."

With every second that elapsed, Courtney feared that Leonard would reappear, and she felt like she was going to pass out. But somehow in the stress of the moment, an idea occurred to her. She had no time to think it through, just to blurt it out.

"I have a plan," she said. She was scared to even say those words ever again, like it would jinx the two of them. None of their plans had worked so far, and this was the most risky, terrifying plan of all. Her tongue felt large and heavy in her mouth. "If you're up for it, it might work."

"Anything."

"I leave you here against the tree. Maybe even tie you back up. And then I wait for Leonard to get back." She paused. "I hide. And I get him with the hatchet."

She could scarcely believe what she was suggesting to Reyna. She wasn't sure it was something she could actually pull off. She also didn't know if Reyna would allow it to happen. Such a plan was filled with the possibility for error, and Courtney didn't know if she herself would agree to it if she were in Reyna's position.

She tore her eyes away from the trees to look back at her friend. For a moment, she didn't know if Reyna could do it, but then Reyna nodded. "Yes. It's the only way. We surprise him."

"We could get killed." The ramifications of the plan were starting to sink in, and Courtney began to waver. "What if he knows I'm here already, or what if I don't hit him hard enough? Then he'll kill both of us."

Without looking at her, Reyna murmured, "We're close to death already. I can feel it." Then she shut her eyes briefly, as though too tired to keep them open anymore. "This is the best plan. It's the smartest. It'll work . . . It has to."

Courtney picked up the ropes again from the snow. They had formed thick, wet, snowy crusts, frayed at the ends where the hatchet had cut through them. To bind Reyna with these ropes made Courtney feel complicit in murder. It seemed like an insane thing to do.

"Faster, faster," Reyna encouraged, and somehow that made it easier. Reyna stood up and staggered against the tree, as Courtney got the ropes back around her. The entire time, both girls were dissecting the forest with their eyes, looking for any movement in the snow, any sign of Leonard. All was still.

Courtney finally got Reyna in position again. She draped the ropes around the back of the tree and retied them loosely, so that maybe Reyna could escape if things went wrong. Her work looked far from perfect, but from a distance, Leonard would hopefully not realize that the ropes had been altered. I just can't let him get too close, Courtney thought.

"I don't want you to leave me," Reyna suddenly said. The words came out in a rush, and it didn't sound like her normal voice at all.

Courtney didn't know what to tell her.

"I shouldn't have said that," Reyna added, her eyes wide.

"I have to go," Courtney said. "It'll be okay, Rey. I'll get him from behind. I won't screw up."

Reyna nodded feebly. "I know." Then suddenly she said, "Wait!"

Courtney stopped.

"It won't work! Your footprints. They're everywhere. He'll see." She struggled against her bonds. "You have to untie me! Make it look like I tried to escape, and the footprints are mine. Or else he'll know."

Courtney understood at once what she meant, and knew they should have thought of it before. She realized she was so scared she wasn't thinking clearly. She undid the ropes, and Reyna fell free again and began crawling around.

Courtney was afraid. "He might kill you when he sees."

"Not yet he won't. He wants me for other things first. . . . He won't kill me."

Courtney wasn't sure, but Reyna was.

"This way I can cover your tracks, or most of them. Go."

Courtney nodded. She backed away in the footprints she'd left when first approaching the tree, trying to swish them away with her feet and hands. She knew the remains of her tracks were all too visible, and might give her away, but Reyna would be her ally. Courtney would have to strike Leonard before he got near the tree and realized someone else had been there. Reyna was still busy crawling around in the snow, trying to obscure everything while protecting her injured arm.

Courtney didn't know what direction Leonard would be coming from, so it was difficult to know where to hide. She had seen some tracks heading north, so she assumed he would be coming back from that direction, but she wasn't certain. Leonard was crazy, but he wasn't stupid, and he had sharp instincts.

There was no time for mental debate. Courtney's thoughts were a hot rush of possibilities. She could crouch almost anywhere in the forest around the clearing and get a view of Reyna and the campsite. But Leonard could arrive from any point. If he came up behind her, then he would kill her. Could she take that risk?

Courtney realized with growing dread that there was only one safe place to hide, and it was a truly awful place, a place she didn't want to go. It was inside the snow cave itself. That was the only location where she would be hidden from any direction, yet still be able to see Leonard approaching through the holes in its sides. Assuming he headed directly for the fire or for Reyna, she could get a jump on him with the hatchet. Of course, if he went for the snow cave first, like he'd done with that other prisoner, it would be a straight-out battle.

Courtney would take her chances. Without breaking stride, she headed for the snow cave, continuing to obscure her tracks as much as she could. The snow rolled and undulated here over uneven ground and brush, so the tracks were not as visible as they might have been on a completely flat surface.

Courtney reached the enclosure and scurried inside. For a frightening moment, she thought she might freak out from claustrophobia, but she didn't. Holding the hatchet, she burrowed into the icy embrace of the cave's snow walls, keeping low to the ground. Through the ring of small holes, she could see outside in almost every direction. She held the weapon tightly as she stared out, waiting for Leonard to return. She had no idea if she would have to wait minutes or hours.

What if Leonard doesn't come back until it's dark? she worried. She didn't know what she'd do then, if it would still be possible to see him. Courtney started to doubt herself. Maybe their plan had been a stupid one. Maybe they should have just run for it. Yet in her heart she knew that Leonard would have found them. After all, hunting was what he was good at, what he liked to do. He would have tortured and killed them at his leisure. Courtney remembered with great clarity what he had done to the other prisoner.

Courtney now wished they had done something to help save that other man, even though he was a murderer too. Had they risked raising their voices, at least he might have conveyed Leonard's true identity. But there had been no chance. Courtney knew that Leonard had made them part of his madness, of his killing spree, probably by design.

Courtney peered out one of the small holes to look at Reyna. The girl was still flailing around near the base of the tree. Courtney was terrified of what she had to do. She felt very far from the person she'd been just a few days ago, as though the fear and insanity of the situation had infected her. But on another level, she also felt stronger. She was starting to realize that she did indeed have it in her to strike Leonard down. It would be like killing a rabid dog.

As she lay in wait, the stress and the cold played tricks on her mind. Crazy snatches of old dialogue between her and Reyna came into her head from all their years of friendship. She never thought they would have got into a situation like this one, that was for sure. She supposed she was glad she was with Reyna at the end. If she died, at least it would be with her friend. She just wished she could see her parents one last time before the curtains closed.

Courtney's biggest fear was that Leonard would somehow know where she was and creep up on the snow cave with the rifle. She knew he could shoot through the snow, assuming he still had bullets, and wound or kill her. She wondered idly why he hadn't just shot them all when he first got the rifle, but maybe the game would have been too easy for him then.

Another unexpected fear popped into her mind: What

if he never planned on coming back? What if this was all part of a sadistic scheme, and he was just going to leave Reyna tied up as food for the wolves? If that was the case, then she and Reyna needed to get out of there as soon as they could, but how would they know? Courtney wasn't sure how long she could wait in the snow cave before she or Reyna froze to death.

What if, what if, Courtney muttered inwardly, sick of her own thoughts. There was no way to predict what Leonard was thinking, or what he would do. His mind wasn't like a normal person's. Like he'd told them himself, psychopaths weren't rational.

The minutes passed slowly because each second contained an entire world of terror. Courtney continued to turn her head, checking the forest in all directions.

And then, Leonard finally appeared.

Courtney heard him before she saw him, the distinct crunching sound of human footsteps coming toward the campsite through the snow. For a moment, she got disoriented and couldn't tell what direction the sound was coming from. Panicked, she twisted around, trying to see through the holes. For a heart-stopping instant, she couldn't see him at all and thought maybe it was too late. But then she caught a glimpse of his borrowed blue jacket through the trees, and realized he was approaching the campsite from her left. He was still a hundred feet or more away.

Courtney tried to keep her breathing as shallow as

possible so that he wouldn't hear her. She hunched down, making herself small, and completely still.

As Leonard got to the edge of the clearing, he came fully into view. The rifle was slung jauntily over his right shoulder, as though he were a hunter coming back from a weekend excursion. What struck Courtney the most was that he seemed completely at peace, and at home in his environment. He looked like a man who knew exactly what he was doing.

But he stopped in total surprise when he looked across the clearing and saw all the footprints, and Reyna floundering near her tree. Courtney tracked Leonard with her eyes as he broke into an edgy, loping run toward her friend. He slowed only when he grew near and perceived that Reyna was not much of a threat.

"Going somewhere?" he called out to her, sounding amused.

Reyna just moaned indecipherable syllables of fear. Courtney hoped she was acting, but couldn't be sure.

"Leaving so soon?" Leonard mocked her. "Be my guest." He lowered the rifle, letting it hang from his hand. "I'll hunt you down like a cottontail, if that's what you really want."

Courtney couldn't hear Reyna's reply. She just kept staring at Leonard's back as he menaced Reyna, trying to get up the courage to move.

"How'd you get free, anyhow?" he was asking Reyna.

"You must be stronger than you look." In another second or two, Courtney knew he would probably check the ropes and start to figure out that Reyna had had some help.

Do it now! the voice in Courtney's head told her suddenly. *While he's busy with Reyna. He won't hear you. Do it right now.*

Courtney was almost surprised to hear the voice tell her those words. She was used to her inner voice always questioning and doubting her, but now it was helping her. Yet it wasn't enough. She felt herself starting to cry out of fear and frustration, but she bit down hard on her lip to make it stop.

If you don't act right now, it will be too late, the voice said calmly. *Leonard will see the ropes have been cut, and he'll kill both of you because he is insane. You have to stop this. You have to take action. No one is going to help you, Courtney. Whether you and Reyna live is up to you—and only you.*

In some ways, it seemed easier to obey the voice than to fight it. Courtney knew the odds against Leonard were not too good. She doubted she was physically strong enough to get in a blow that would kill him. It was pretty likely that she would hit him with the hatchet, maybe wound him, and then he'd turn around and blow her away with the rifle. Yet the alternative to action was just as bad, because she and Reyna would die anyway out here. At least this way they would recapture control of their own fate for a moment.

Courtney said a silent, inward prayer in the second

before she left the snow cave to attack Leonard. It was nothing complex or religious, and she didn't know if she was praying to God, or to Elliot, or to herself. It was just this:

I don't want to die.

I'm not ready yet.

So please don't let me die.

Then she sucked in her breath and tightened her grip on the hatchet.

Courtney didn't take her eyes off Leonard's shoulder blades as she emerged from her shelter, holding the hatchet firmly in both hands like a baseball bat. She walked deliberately, but quietly and slowly, placing one foot down and then the other. If Leonard hadn't been occupied with tormenting Reyna, he probably would have heard her coming.

Courtney bore down on him, her eyes now fixed on a point just below his neck. She knew she would only have one chance, at best. If she swung the hatchet and missed, that would be the end of everything. She felt like she was no longer breathing at all.

Leonard was just twenty paces away. He was laughing and looking at Reyna as she tried to get up from the snow. He put a foot on her chest and kicked her back down, completely caught up in the thrill of his cruelty. Courtney didn't know if Reyna could see her coming or not, but she realized it was best if Reyna didn't. She was afraid the look in Reyna's eyes might give the surprise away.

These thoughts and a thousand more raced through her mind in the few seconds as she got closer. Now she was fifteen paces away, now twelve. She raised the hatchet high in the air. Any doubts about whether she could strike another person had long since evaporated.

It's him or us, and I choose us, she told herself.

Suddenly Leonard stopped laughing, and to her horror, he tilted his head back like he'd heard her. Courtney knew if Leonard turned around, or even just caught a glimpse of her somehow, he would start shooting. Reyna began screaming and clutching at Leonard's legs, trying to distract him, and Courtney realized her friend had seen her. But almost in slow motion, she saw Leonard begin to move, his shoulders and torso swiveling around to check out what was coming up behind him. In another instant, the rifle would be pointing at her and firing.

Courtney realized that her time was up, and it didn't matter if she made noise anymore. She hurtled forward through the snow, covering the remaining paces in a blaze of speed. Her mouth was open and she was screaming, but she was barely aware of it.

Leonard turned around, stepping away from Reyna, who was still trying to grab his ankle, with a shocked look on his face. He was trying to bring the rifle up to fire, but his surprise made him sluggish.

The hatchet reached him before he could get the rifle all the way up. Courtney struck him as hard as she had struck anything ever in her life. The hatchet blade buried itself deep into the front part of his chest and neck, just between his collarbones, at a forty-five-degree angle. The blow reverberated down the length of the hatchet and into Courtney's hands. There was a huge concussive blast as the rifle fired, the bullet tearing past Courtney's shoulder and slamming harmlessly into the snow. Leonard twisted backward, wrenching the handle away from her, the hatchet still in his chest. The rifle fell out of his hand and down to the snow.

He staggered back a few paces, his head bent down like he was trying to figure out what had just happened to him. There was surprisingly little blood, just a thin trickle that spattered down the front of his jacket. Courtney was afraid he would yank the hatchet back out, but he seemed to be in a daze. She knew the wound was very deep; she had felt its force.

Courtney stood there, her ears ringing, thinking, *I did it, I did it!* Reyna was yelling excitedly at her from behind Leonard. At the same time, she heard a strange rumbling noise from somewhere in the distance, but she didn't know what it was and she didn't care, so it was easy to ignore.

Leonard finally raised his head and looked at her. He opened his mouth and some bright red blood came out one of the corners. The hatchet remained sticking out of him, like the misplaced turnkey on a wind-up toy. He walked a few more paces away, sideways, like a crab. Courtney was surprised he was still able to move.

From the corner of her eye, she saw Reyna crawling

rapidly toward the discarded rifle. Leonard noticed too, but realized that he couldn't make it in time. He didn't look angry. More than anything, Courtney thought he looked puzzled. He brought his hands up to feel the handle of the hatchet and some understanding came into his eyes.

By the time he took his hands away again, Reyna had the rifle and was sitting in the snow, unsteadily pointing it at him with her remaining hand. A finger was on the trigger, and her damaged limb supported the barrel.

Leonard had lost the power of speech. More blood kept coming out of his mouth as he opened and closed it. Reyna held the gun up higher, taking aim at his chest. She was crying and laughing at the same time, hysterical, but now her good hand seemed steadier.

The strange background rumbling noise grew louder, and Courtney strained to understand it. Slowly, it resolved into the unmistakable sound of a helicopter somewhere in the skies above them. It was the first such noise they had heard during the entire trip. It seemed like a blessing they should hear it now, as well as a horrible irony. Neither Courtney nor Reyna wanted to look up and try to see the helicopter, because that meant they would have to look away from Leonard. *Oh God, please let them see us,* Courtney willed.

Leonard heard the noise too, and he didn't like it. He began backing away from Courtney and Reyna, moving slowly because of his wound. He still wore a look of stupefaction, like he couldn't believe things had turned out this way for him. It was clear that despite the hatchet sticking out of him, he hadn't fully intended on giving up, but the helicopter was a final blow to his plans. Courtney watched him, his gray-blue eyes fixed on hers. He didn't say a word. He just kept moving backward in the snow, using his hands on either side to guide him like a blind man.

Reyna tracked him with the rifle. Leonard saw her, but he didn't try to say or do anything to protect himself. He just kept moving. Courtney wasn't sure whether she wanted Reyna to fire the rifle or not. A large part of her did, because although Leonard was no longer a threat to them, he deserved to die for what he'd done.

Reyna took aim through the gun's site. Courtney prepared for the inevitable loud crack of a gunshot, but Reyna didn't do it.

"Bang!" she yelled instead. And then she started sobbing, deep, hard sobs that shook her whole body. "Bang, you crazy fuck." She still didn't fire at Leonard.

The noise of the helicopter blades now drowned out any other sound, but still, Courtney didn't look up until Leonard had disappeared into the white forest. One second he was still there, partially hidden by snow and branches, and the next he was completely gone, leaving a narrow trail of blood. Only then did Courtney tilt her head back and upward.

There was a rescue helicopter above them and to the left, hanging in the gray sky. It was white, with a police search-and-rescue insignia painted in red on its belly. To

Courtney's utter surprise, she thought she could faintly see Harris leaning out one of the passenger windows and waving frantically. His wide, familiar face came as an unexpected relief. The police must have taken him along to help guide them, Courtney thought, as she struggled to wave back. Or maybe they had just recently found him too. Reyna managed to get over to her side, swaying from fatigue, still holding the rifle.

Courtney was glad she hadn't shot Leonard. Reyna had held his life in her hands, but she had taken the moral path. If she'd killed him, it would have brought them down to his level. Now they were not tainted by him, and he had not destroyed who they were. They were free.

There wasn't much room for the helicopter to land in the clearing, but somehow it was skillfully piloted downward until it reached the ground. It landed on a flat patch of snow near the two girls. Courtney and Reyna huddled with their backs to it, because the blades were whipping up a barrage of ice and snow. With the blades still turning, men in uniform leaped out of the helicopter and rushed to help get them on board.

Everything happened very fast. Courtney and Reyna were hustled inside before either of them knew what was going on. Courtney tried to speak to one of the men and warn him about Leonard, but he was busy checking her vital signs and wouldn't listen. Another man was tending to Reyna. He had very carefully taken the rifle away from her. Courtney wondered if these men would go after Leonard too, or if somehow they hadn't seen him.

It felt warm inside the helicopter to Courtney. Within a minute, they were back up in the air, hovering above the clearing and the trees. Courtney felt like her heart was overwhelmed with hope, but also with sorrow. She knew she and Reyna would have to tell everyone about Jeremy, and the truth about Leonard's identity. But there would be time for all of that soon enough. She looked over at Reyna and said, "We made it," and Reyna smiled back.

There was a final surprise from the helicopter, one Courtney knew she would never forget. As they moved upward and away from the campsite, Courtney looked down through the window and saw a small, blood-drenched figure in the snow. It was Leonard. The hatchet was gone, and Courtney realized he must have finally pulled it out of himself. But Leonard was not alone.

It took Courtney a moment to understand what she was seeing, until she realized the wolf pack had found him, and he was running with them, like an injured quarterback making the big play. He weaved and darted and so did the animals, pacing him, anticipating his movements. They nipped at him as they ran, and he screamed. She couldn't hear his screams, of course, she could only see that he was screaming by the way his head bent back and his mouth opened up in agony. The wolves were opening and closing their mouths too.

Courtney held Reyna's good hand as the two of them leaned over and watched Leonard get taken down to the snow by the wolves. The number of wolves around him grew until his body was barely visible through the fur and the teeth and the vicious, scrabbling claws. The wolves seemed to be carrying him away. Courtney realized that when the police came looking for him later, they probably wouldn't have much luck. She guessed they would not find his body until spring, when the first thaw came, if then. Very little would be left of him.

The helicopter angled out of view and abruptly they were flying over oceans of white treetops. One of the uniformed men tried to help Courtney sit back, but she pushed him away to keep watching. There was no sign that anything lived down there below them anymore, in the snow and ice. Everything down there looked frozen and cold. But I'm alive, Courtney told herself, the clattering of the helicopter rotors loud in her ears. Nature had not claimed her. She felt the presence of Reyna and Harris close beside her, and the medics.

Harris was saying something: "Jesus, look at you two!" he yelled. "What happened out there?! Where's Jeremy? He's not with you? Listen, Mel's okay, she's at the hospital—"

Courtney couldn't hear the rest. *So we're alive. Except for Jeremy, we all made it through.* She knew she would mourn for Jeremy later, when she allowed the force of the loss to hit her. But she wasn't ready for that pain yet.

Courtney shut her eyes and leaned her head back on the seat, tired beyond comprehension. They had beaten Leonard. She felt as though she was temporarily at peace, and it was a very unlikely feeling. She did not feel as young as she once had.

In the last few days, she had been through a more vivid experience than anything she could have imagined. She knew that life would be okay now, that she would return to all the familiar people and things she loved.

Courtney opened her eyes again and gazed down at the white pine tops that rushed past beneath them. The forest was so vast, it seemed endless, as though it stretched out forever. She could see no limits or boundaries to it, no matter how far she looked.

Courtney wondered what it would feel like to get away from this cold world, and back home to her family. She guessed it would feel good.